PERSONALITY MURDERS

Personality Murders

Christina H Lamb

* * * * *

1

PERSONALITY MURDERS

PERSONALITY MURDERS

TABLE OF CONTENTS

INTRODUCTION

It is a hot, muggy, August morning in 1990. Eighteen year old Paul Montgomery is off to start a new life in a new town. His new home is a place called Pansy House, located in Bryn Mawr, Pennsylvania.

House, a place for teens and young adults with mental illness to learn how to be self-sufficient in their own place and in the world. Paul's parents are hoping he works on his temper and anger issues. Little do they know that their hopes and dreams are shattered the day they met a girl who will destroy their lives and the lives around her. Her kind, calm nature is a cover-up for an inner, deep, cold darkness within her heart and soul. A young woman, whom trouble, chaos and conflict follow where ever she goes.

SATURDAY, AUGUST 4, 1990

18-year-old Paul Montgomery is nervous and excited as his parents drive him an 1 ½ hr. to a mental health group called Pansy House. Paul has never been away from his family, nor at a place where he knows no one. His thoughts are all over. What kind of friends would he make? What kind of life would he have? Would Marie change her mind about dating him once he gets out? All these thoughts and more are running in his mind. On the other hand, Paul is excited to be able to make his own decisions. All he has to do is follow the rules.

The ride from Pottstown to Bryn Mawr was long. They kept busy by looking at the beautiful scenery, the different restaurants and stores. The odd named towns. When they finally got there, they nearly jumped out of the car altogether. Their legs were stiff from sitting so long.

Pansy House consisted of 4 buildings, 2 for guys and 2 for girls. Each building has 6 floors. 5 of the floors have 5 bedrooms with their own bathrooms. The rooms have 2 double beds, 2 dressers and 2 closets. Each room has cable tv and internet service. The first floor has a large eat-in kitchen where each one is responsible for storing, cooking and eating their own food. The living room has a big tv on each side of the room, 4 couches and 3 chairs. Each building has an office with 2 staff members. The outside was brick with a wraparound porch and a huge yard for cook-outs.

As they approached the front door, an older woman about in her 40's, with long black hair, met them at the door.

"Hello!! My name is Juniper Kinkade. I am the director of Pansy House. And you must be the Montgomery's."

"My name is Bob, Paul's dad, and this is Paul's mom, Kym Plumber."

It's nice to meet you all. If you will follow me to my office. There is some paperwork that needs to be filled out. Then I will go over the rules and what is expected of Paul and show you his room."

It took an hour to go through all the paperwork, rules and expectations. Then they were shown Paul's room and helped him unpack his stuff. Paul walked his parents to the door to say goodbye. As they were leaving, a young woman was standing on the porch of the boy's side. Tiffany Powers, a 19-year-old who was a bit on the heavy side, she was very kind and welcoming. She looks like Marie, the woman of Paul's dreams.

"You must be new! My name is Tiffany Powers. I stay in the Purple House over there on the right. Who are you and where are you from?"

"I'm Paul Montgomery and these are my parents, Bob and Kym. I am from Pottstown."

As Tiffany shakes Paul's hand, he imagines himself being with Marie. Everything about Tiffany reminds him of Marie. Her black hair, her gorgeous smile that goes ear to ear.

The tenderness of her voice. It wasn't until Tiffany says, "Nice to meet you. I'm from Norristown." That snaps Paul back to reality.

"Well, we need to get moving to avoid rush hour traffic. Call me anytime." "O.k. bye mom, bye dad! I love you!"

The car ride home was so quiet, you could hear a pin drop. Neither Bob nor Kym knew where to start. Bob broke the silence first.

"So what do you think of all this?"

"Well, Juniper and the staff seem nice, the house is very homey and welcoming. That girl Tiffany seems like a lovely girl. I just hope Paul follows the rules and gets his life on track."

"Yeah I agree with you. But he is an adult now, all we can do is pray. Don't you think that

Tiffany looks a lot like Marie?" 10

"Yes I do. That has me a little worried. I hope everything he put Marie through, he doesn't do to this girl. If they get together."

"So Tiffany, tell me about yourself."

"What would you like to know?"

Like, are you dating, how old are you, what do you like to do?"

"Well, I am 19 and am 2 months pregnant. My boyfriend's name is Jose. We are part of a band that is held in the attic here 3 times a week. I am the lead singer. Joe is the drummer, someone plays the keyboard and another friend plays the guitar. Stick with me and I will show you the ropes."

"Thanks! I am 18, I play a little guitar. I am not that good though. I never had a girlfriend.

I'm glad to be on my own."

"So, why are you here? What is your illness?" Tiffany asks.

"I have Asperger's and I have anger issues. I am here because I've been getting into trouble at home. And I've been stalking this girl I want to date, but she doesn't like me like that. She's married. So, what about you? What are you here for?"

"I have Bipolar Manic depression, anxiety and depression. I've been on my own since my 16th birthday. Everywhere I've lived, bad things happen, and they always blame me when all I tried to do is to help people out."

"Sorry to hear that."

"Well, it's 8:00, curfew is at 9:00. We can chat another time."

"Can we hang out some time?"

"Maybe."

Before leaving for the night, Juniper approaches Paul and asks how his first day went. Paul tells her about his new friend Tiffany and how she said he could hang with her. When he told her, Juniper had a frightened look on her face. She tried to warn him, but Paul just laughed and went to his room."

That night, Paul could not sleep. He could not stop thinking about Tiffany. The new girl for him. Everything about her reminded him of Marie. Since Marie didn't want him, this one would. He thought about helping her raise her baby. Them getting married. Him telling Marie, sorry too late. His thoughts were interrupted by the alarm clock. Paul got up, he ate breakfast, did his chore and headed outside to find Tiffany. Before he gets out the door, his roommate Pete stops him to introduce himself.

"Hey, Paul, wait up! I'm your room mate Pete. Would you like to meet some of the guys?

It will only take a minute."

"Nah, not right now! I'm looking for Tiffany, do you know where she is?"

"Dude, you have to be careful with her."

Not listening, Paul darts out the door and heads to the house Tiffany lives in. As he approaches the door, Pete catches up with him and reminds him of the rule.

"Yo! Paul, there's a rule here that says boys are not allowed on the girls side and vice versa, without permission from staff."

I just wanted to hang with Tiffany."

"Look, you need to be careful with her. Come hang with me and the guys."

(sighing) "Fine!"

"Hey guys, let me introduce you to the new guy Paul! The guy in the cast is Lucky. He is leaving in a few months. The one playing air drums is Jose, Tiffanie's boyfriend. He is the band's drummer. The guy with his hair slicked back is Roberto, he plays the keyboard. He is also the guy to go to if you need a date. The dude yelling on his cell phone is Ralph. He plays the guitar. He can get you anything you need. I play guitar also. If you need to borrow anything, ask."

"Nice to meet you all. Can anyone spare any food until my dad gets here?"

"Do you like Ramen Noodles? I can spare 12."

"Thanks Pete. When my dad comes up, I will have him replace them."

"No problem."

"So, Paul, I hear you already met my girl Tiffany. Isn't she hot?"

(Blushing) "Ummmm.... Yeah, sure."

"Don't get any ideas, she is mine."

"Hey!! Leave the new kid alone!" Lucky breaks in.

(Roberto Butts in) "Hey, new kid, what's your story?"

"What do you mean by my story?"

"Like where are you from? Why are you here? Tell us about you."

"I'm from Pottstown. I like to skateboard, play guitar, and hang out. I have Asperger's and anger issues. I've been getting into trouble at home and I stalked this girl I like who is married."

"Kool!"

Since it was a beautiful day out, they decided to stay on the porch. They all filled Paul in on whose who. Who can be trusted. How to get around the rules. Where the best hang out spots are. Who to watch out for. They gave him a map on how to get around town. They all had a good time getting to know each other better. For the first time Paul had friends who seemed to really like him.

After the guys left, Paul remained on the porch. He laid on the hammock, eyes closed with the sun beating down on him. Fantasizing about Tiffany and Marie. How, one way or the other, one of them would be his. He wondered what they were wearing, what they were doing, who they were hanging out with. His thoughts were interrupted by yelling and screaming from the girls house next door.

"WHO THE HELL DO YOU THINK YOU ARE? YOU THINK YOU ARE SO BIG AND BAD, YOU ARE ALL TALK AND NO ACTION." Yells Jenn, a friend of Tiffanies.

"I'LL SHOW YOU WHO IS ALL TALK!"

Tiffany grabs Jenn's hair. Both girls were hitting each other, yelling and screaming at each other.

"JUST BECAUSE YOU ARE BIGGER THAN ME, DOESN'T MEAN YOU CAN BEAT

ME!!!!" Yell's Tiffany.

"IS THAT ALL YOU GOT TIFFANY? YOU DIRTY WHORE."

"YOU'RE CALLING ME A WHORE? WHO IS THE ONE SLEEPING WITH HER BEST

FRIENDS MAN?"

Jenn pushes Tiffany so hard she falls down the stairs. The police are called, they arrive with paramedics, the boys from next door all run to see what was going on. Jose sees Tiffany being taken out by the paramedics. His heart starts racing, he begins to cry and yells.

"TIFFANY!!! TIFFANY!!"

"Sir, you have to stand back!"

"That's my girlfriend, she's pregnant."

"O.k., you can ride with the paramedics."

"Thank you!'

Officer Menendez walks over to Jenn, to find out what happened.

"Ma'am, my name is Officer Menendez, I want you to start at the beginning and tell me what happened."

"I was walking to my room when I heard Tiffany talking about some girl thinking she's all that. I got closer to her door and heard her say, "Jenn thinks she's all that because she can get guys. When they only want her because she's easy. She tries to dress like me because she knows I rock my clothes. She looks like a .10 cent whore. I only hang with her to be nice. I can't stand her." So, I kicked her door in, and the fight was on. I didn't mean to push her down the stairs, I just wanted her to stop pulling my hair."

"O.k. I need you to come down to the station with me to make a statement. There may be charges pressed against you. Can a staff member come along to take you home, if needed?"

"I will get one."

At Lincoln General Emergency room, Tiffany is asked what happened as the doctor drew blood and ran some tests. Just to make sure nothing was broken and to make sure the baby is o.k.

"Ms. Powers, my name is Officer Winfield. Start at the beginning and tell me what happened."

"Honestly, Officer, I don't know why she attacked me. I was sitting in my room, chatting with my friend on the phone. When out of nowhere my door gets kicked in, Jenn starts hitting me, yelling and screaming. I hit her back in self-defense. She drags me to the stairs and throws me down the stairs."

"You did nothing to provoke Miss Crumbs?"

"No Officer, I didn't provoke her in any way."

"When you are done here, I need you to come downtown to give a full statement,"

"Sure, no problem."

As Officer Winfield was leaving the room, Dr. Potts came in to go over the tests that were performed.

"Dr. I am Officer Winfield. Can you give me a status on her condition?"

"Well, she only suffered some minor bumps and bruises."

"And the baby?"

"Miss Powers was never pregnant."

"WOW!"

"Can I see my patient now?"

"Sure."

"Miss Powers, I am Dr. Potts, how are you feeling?"

"I feel o.k. How is the baby?"

"That's what I wanted to talk to you about. All the tests we performed indicate you were never pregnant."

"SHH! I don't want my boyfriend to know."

"I am not lying for you."

"I didn't say to lie, just don't offer the information. Let me tell him."

"Do you promise to tell him?"

"Yes, of course."

"Now, for the rest of the other tests. Other than some minor bumps and bruises, everything looks good. The nurse will bring you the discharge papers." As Jose walks in, Tiffany begins to cry.

"Hey, is everything ok hon? How's the baby?"

"Jose, sit down. I have some bad news to tell you. I lost the baby."

They both held each other closely, trying to comfort one another, reassuring one another that it will be ok. That they can try again. The nurse walked in puzzled as to why they were crying when there was nothing wrong. She went over the discharge papers and released Tiffany.

When they arrive at the police station, Jose sees Jenn and starts yelling.

"MURDERER!!!!! ARREST HER, SHE KILLED MY BABY!"

"Sir, I know you are upset. Please let us do our job."

"Well Officer Winfield, Arrest that woman! She killed my unborn child"

"Sir, according to the report from the emergency room doctor, Miss Powers was never pregnant."

"Your lying, she was 2 months pregnant. I saw the ultrasound pictures, show them Tiff!"

"Let me read you the report we got. Results for Tiffany Powers, age 19. Blood test, negative. Urine test, negative, ultrasound, negative. There is nothing showing Miss

Powers was ever pregnant."

"That's not possible. I saw the ultrasound picture of the baby with my own eyes. How could she fake an ultrasound? Unless.... you took it from someone."

"Jose, don't believe them. They are lying to you. Jenn must've changed the results. You know how jealous of me she is!"

"Stop it Tiff! How could you do this to me or anyone? I'm tired of all the drama. I'm tired of the mood swings. You have lied to me and humiliated me for the last time. WE are over!"

"We can make this work. I promise I won't lie or hurt you ever again. Please give me one more chance? I will see a therapist. I will do whatever you say. PLEASE!!!!" Begs Tiffany.

"I want nothing more to do with you. We are through!"

Jose pushes Tiffany away as he leaves the police station slamming the door, hurt and angry.

"Miss Powers, I understand you are having a bad day, I need you to read your statement. If any changes need to be made, we will make them. If not, sign it and you are free to go. The same for you Miss Crumbs, read and sign."

They signed their statements and left. Both girls sat apart from one another on the way home. Neither one said anything to each other. The van was quiet until Juniper says to them....

"I hope you both are proud of yourselves. You not only made yourselves look bad, you made Pansy House look bad as well. You both are on restriction. No friends over, you cannot leave the premises. You can only sit on the porch."

"That's not fair! It's all Jenn's fault. I did nothing wrong!"."

"Me? You were trash talking me. I had a right to defend myself."

"ENOUGH! You both are at fault. The restriction remains for 2 weeks."

"2 weeks! We will miss the co-ed dance."

"Maybe that will teach you both to control yourselves." Tiffany leans over to Jenn and says.

"Watch your back. I will get even with you."

"Bring it!"

The rest of the ride home was a quiet one. Both girls were angry that they would be missing the dance. Everyone went to bed. All were exhausted.

SUNDAY, AUGUST 5, 1990

The next day the guys were concerned about Tiffany and went to see how she was doing.

"Yo! Jose, how is Tiffany doing? Asked Ralph.

"I don't want to discuss her."

"Everything alright?"

"I said I don't want to discuss Tiffany. GET OFF MY BACK!!"

"Look man, we're just concerned that's all."

"I'm sorry, I know you guys mean well. Tiffany and Jenn are okay. I found out that Tiffany was never pregnant."

"WOW! Sorry to hear that. If you need someone to talk to, your boys are here for ya."

"Thanks, bro. I don't want the new kid to know."

"No problem, bro."

"Thanks."

Tiffany was deep in thought as she sat on the porch. She was thinking of ways to get even with Jenn. It's her fault I lost the love of my life. She thought maybe she would scare her. Then she decided that wasn't good enough. Her inner demons begin to take over her thoughts. No longer was she in control. They began to speak to her like another person was holding a conversation with her. The one called the Evil one did most of the talking.

"I know just what to do! She will never bother you again!!"

As Tiffany was talking to herself and was deep in thought, she didn't notice Paul walking towards her.

"Hey Tiffany!!" 19

(Startled) Tiffany says, "Um... um.. What's your name again?"

"It's Paul, the new guy next door. We met a few days ago."

" Oh yeah, right! I remember, sorry. You startled me. I was deep in thought."

"Are you okay?"

"Well, no." When Jenn pushed me down the stairs, I lost the baby and Jose left me."

"Sorry to hear that." I'm here for you."

" Thanks. And I'm on restriction for what she did to me. It's not fair!" (She cries)

"Don't cry, it will be alright. I can't believe she got you into trouble for something you didn't do. If I was a girl, I would beat her up."

"Really?? You would do that for me?"

"Yes! I would do anything for you. I think you are beautiful." The wheels of the Evil one began to turn.

"Hmmmmm... This will be easier than I thought. Now to figure out when, where and how. And it's bye Jenn. Paul will be the one to blame."

"I know you are going through a rough time right now, with losing the baby and Jose all in one day. I was wondering would you ever consider going out with me?"

"I don't know. I'm still in love with Jose."

"Can you think about it? I gotta head back. We are planning for that stupid dance."

"You don't want to go?"

"Nah, I don't know how to dance, and I don't have anyone to go with. I will look stupid sitting by myself."

"If I was going, you could dance with me."

"Why aren't you going?"

"I'm on restriction. I can't go."

Angrily, Paul says, "That girl needs a beat down for all the trouble she caused. Well, I have to get back."

"If you see Jose, ask him to come over."

"Sure, no problem."

At the dance meeting, everyone was getting excited, making suggestions for the big dance. They figured out what kind of beverages and snacks they would get. Who would be the DJ?"

The girls are responsible for the decorations and setting up. The boys are taking care of everything else. Paul sat there unnoticed. No one bothered to ask him his opinion.

As soon as the meeting was over, Paul decided to take a walk at the park. It was a beautiful day out. He loves to look up at the peaceful sky with white billowing clouds.

The gorgeous tree with white and pink flowers. He sat on a bench, taking in the scenery. He stayed at the park for an hour. Then he headed back to Pansy House. On his way home, he saw Jose and ran to catch him.

" Jose, wait up, dude. Hey, Jose! Stop!"

"WHAT PAUL?" I'm taking a walk to clear my head."

"Look man ,I just wanted to tell you how sorry I am for your loss."

"My loss? Oh, you mean losing the baby?"

"Yes, Tiffany told me, she also said she wants to see you."

"I just can't stand to look at her right now."

"You can't blame her for something Jenn did. That ain't right."

"Paul, you have no clue what you are talking about. There is more to this than you know. For your own safety, stay out of it!"

"If I got it all wrong, then tell me. Don't threaten me for trying to be nice."

"That wasn't a threat. I'm trying to warn you. That's all I am telling you right now."

"I'm not trying to stick my nose in your business, I was trying to be a friend."

"Let's just drop it and move on. Friends?"

"Friends! Hey, let's hang out sometime."

The 2 go their separate ways. At the girls' house, Tiffany goes to get some paper and pen to write her plan of revenge on Jenn down. And how to make it look like Paul did it.

On the top of both pages: "Revenge on Jenn plan." The Evil one thought it best to make 2 copies. Tiffany's copy to be burned when everything was all done. The second one she would trick Paul into hiding for her in his room. The plan would be as follows:

When: during co-ed dance.

Where: on the grounds.

How: The day of the dance,the Evil one will sneak into Jenn's room, loosen the bolts of the ceiling fan above her bed. That way when she turns on the fan it will kill Jenn on impact. Now all we need to do is have Paul hide the plan in his room. And to plan how to get something from Paul to plant at the murder scene. Something everyone had seen, but something he won't miss. For this to work, Tiffany needs to pretend to date Paul and the manipulator needs to create an argument between Paul and Jenn.

" I know just how to do it." Chimes in the manipulator.

"Good! I want it to go smoothly! No mistakes."

" Gotcha!!"

That night everyone slept well. Some were getting excited about the dance and who they would be dancing with. Paul dreamt of Tiffany and Marie. He tossed and turned as he pictured himself with each of them and how their life would be. Then he woke up in a cold sweat. And stayed up thinking the whole night.

Monday, August 6, 1990

It was a dark, rainy Monday. Five days until the dance. The boys are ordering the food, beverages, and the DJ. The girls were putting the decorations together. The Evil one is already to go. It's all up to the manipulator now.

Paul received a text from an unknown number.

"Hey, Paul, meet me at the corner in 10 minutes."

"Who is this?"

"You will find out when you get there. Oh, don't tell anyone where you are going." "Okay I won't."

When Paul reaches the corner, he notices that it is Tiffany.

"What is going on? Why all the secrecy??"

"Not so loud! I'm not supposed to leave the grounds, I'm on restriction until Monday.

Remember!"

"Sorry! I forgot!"

"It's okay. The reason I asked you here is to ask you if you still want to date me?"

"YES!!! YES!!"

"Well, I thought about it, and my answer is yes."

"Wait, do you mean, yes as in the future you would consider dating me or you want to date now?"

"I mean let's date now."

"REALLY???"

"Yes, really!!"

"Now, go back to the house, and don't tell anyone we are dating."

"What am I to say when they see me excited?"

"Tell them you're dating the girl you stalked."

"The girl I stalked. What if they don't believe me?"

"How will they know if you're telling the truth or not?"

"Ok, I will say Marie."

"Good now go back ahead of me."

Paul was so excited he was beaming from ear to ear. His face lit up like the stars shining in the sky. He couldn't wait to tell his friends and family.

"Hello!"

"Hey, dad, guess what?"

"What Paul?"

"I am dating Tiffany now."

"That's good. Doesn't she date some other guy and is pregnant?"

"Well here's the thing. She lost the baby in a fight with a girl. And Jose left her."

"Sorry to hear that."

"Can I call you back, dad; I want to tell Aunt Joan."

"Congratulations son."

"What Paul?"

"Aunt Joan, I got good news!"

"I finally got a girlfriend!"

"That's good. What's her name?"

"This girl Tiffany. She lives on the girls side. You'll like her, Aunt Joan. She sings like

Marie and has a big mouth like you."

" That's nice. Can you send me a pic of her?"

"No problem, Aunt Joan. Can you tell my mom and everyone else for me?"

"Sure, no problem."

They both hung up. Joan gathers everyone together to tell them Paul's good news.

"Hey Kym, can you gather everyone up for me? I had a call from Paul and wanted to tell everyone at the same time."

"Now what? I'm an Important person." Says Sam, who is Paul's stepdad.

"I just got a call from Paul. He is dating a girl named Tiffany." "Bob and I met her when we dropped Paul off." Adds Kym.

"Where is she from?" asks Sam.

"All I know is she lives in the Pansy House. And from the pic I just got from Paul, she looks a lot like Marie."

"Why doesn't he leave me alone?"

"Let's not panic. Marie, it's a good thing he found some-one. This is an answer to prayer."

"At least he won't be obsessed with you anymore. Although it is creepy that she looks like you, Marie." Adds Brandon, Marie's husband.

Paul was beaming from ear to ear as he entered the house. The guys were getting ready to watch a movie when Paul walked in.

"Looks like someone is having a good day!" Declares Lucky. "Umm... Yeah! This girl I'm in love with finally said she will date me." "That's good, bro! What's her name again? Asked Lucky.

"Marie Kwon."

"Wait! Isn't she married?" Asks Pete.

"She said she wants to see me on the side to see if it will work between us before she ends her marriage."

"Well, be careful man. Hey, we are going to watch a movie. Come join us."

"What movie?"

"It's called Candy Man."

"Alright, let me get some snacks and a drink."

"Hurry up! We want to get started."

"Alright!"

All through the movie Paul couldn't stop thinking about Tiffany, his first girlfriend. Her gorgeous smile, how she wears her long black hair. How much she looks like Marie. How he couldn't wait to be alone with her. His thoughts were interrupted when one of the guys poured a glass of ice cold water on his head.

"What the hell did you do that for, Ralph?"

"Because you were daydreaming too loudly."

"Sorry! I was thinking of Ti.... I mean Marie." "That's obvious!

"Look! I said I was sorry. Now leave me alone."

"Chill out, man! I was just messing with you."

"I'm going to take a shower."

"You need to check that attitude and get over yourself."

"I have an attitude! You're an ass. You started it."

"Wanna take this outside?"

"Let's do it right here."

"Let's see what you got!"

"Cool it! Both of you! If you're caught fighting, you both will be on lockdown," says Pete.

"Whatever! Just stay away from me, Paul."

That night, the house was peaceful. Paul fell asleep as soon as his head hit the pillow. He dreamt about being married to Tiffany. The dream felt so real, he thought it was really happening. Tiffany wore a white pearl necklace with matching earrings. Her bouquet was white and pink carnations with white baby's breath, Her maid of honor and bridesmaids wore light pink dresses with dangly silver earrings and a beautiful diamond heart necklace. The flower girl was his sister, Lynn. She wore a white lacy dress with a silver heart locket. In her basket are red rose petals. The groom, best man and groomsmen wore black tuxedos. The groom had a pink carnation on his tuxedo. The guys wore white carnations. He woke up in a wet bed. He quickly got up and changed his bedding before his roommate, Pete woke up. Then he went downstairs for breakfast.

Tuesday, August 7, 1990

A new day, Tuesday, 4 days until the dance. The girls were all setting up the decorations at the social hall, except Jenn and Tiffany. Both girls sat on the porch. Neither one said a word to each other. Tiffany starts to text Paul.

Tiffany's inner demons began to scheme. The manipulator tells the Evil one to, "Watch him work his magic."

The Evil one says, "Just get the damn job done." "Hey sexy!" Texted Tiffany.

"Hey Tiff, what's up?"

"Nothing, just chilling on the porch with Jenn."

"Jenn?"

"Don't worry, we aren't even speaking to each other."

"If she starts, tell me, I will be right over."

"I promise."

As Tiffany is texting Paul, Jenn starts a conversation with her.

"Tiffany, can we talk?"

"What, Jenn?"

"Look, I'm sorry for what I've done to you. I didn't want you to lose Jose. I just wanted to shut you up."

"Well, I did lose Jose. But it was my fault for lying. I'm sorry for the things I said about you. Let's start over."

"Sounds good to me."

"HELP ME! HELP ME! She's hurting me." Tiffany texts to Paul.

"I'm on my way."

"Are we friends, Jenn?"

"Friends, Tiff." 25

Jenn gave Tiffany a tight hug as Paul came running towards the porch. He sees what looks like Jenn choking Tiffany. He runs up on the porch, grabs Jenn by the arm, swings her into the banister of the porch, bruising her lower back. He begins to shake her and is yelling......

"GET OFF HER!! HAVEN'T YOU DONE ENOUGH TO HER?"

Pushing Paul away, "I was only giving her a hug."

"Don't you ever hurt Tiffany again. So help me. I will get you."

"What are you talking about? I didn't hurt her. I did nothing wrong."

"Anyone would have done the same thing in my spot. If you hurt her again, what I will do to you won't be an accident."

Hearing the commotion, the kids all gathered around to see what was going on. The yelling gets louder.

"TIFFANY!!! Don't just stand there. PLEASE tell Paul the truth!"

"She was hugging me so hard I couldn't breathe."

"That's a lie! I wasn't hurting Tiffany. It was just a hug."

"Tiffany wouldn't lie to me. Don't ever put your hands on her again. This is your only warning. "

"Paul, Tiffany and I were making amends." "What is going on here?" Asks Juniper.

"Jenn. Choked Tiffany. I saw it with my own eyes."

"I was not choking her; I was giving her a hug. We were making amends."

"Don't believe her! I saw everything! "

"ALRIGHT! ENOUGH! I want to hear from Tiffany. Tiffany, what happened?"

"Well, Jenn and I were making amends and as we were hugging, Paul comes running up on the porch. He grabbed Jenn by the arm and started yelling at Jenn. I tried to stop him. He saw Jenn hugging me and thought she was choking me." "So, you're saying it was a misunderstanding? Is that true, Jenn and Paul." "Yes, Juniper, that's true." Says Jenn.

"Well I don't know. I got a text from Tiffany saying to help her that Jenn is hurting her.

See, I still have the texts."

"Alright! I heard enough! The texts do show that Tiffany did tell Paul Jenn was hurting her. So, Jenn you are not in any trouble this time. Tiffany, you get 2 extra days. Paul, you will not be allowed to attend the dance. Anymore between you girls and a stricter restriction will be set. Did you hear me?"

All 3 said, "we hear you."

"Jenn!"

"Yes, Paul."

"I'm sorry, I honestly thought you were choking Tiffany."

"It's not your fault Tiffany started trouble."

"I didn't start trouble! I can't help it that he can't take a joke."

"You didn't even try to stop me."

"How could I, you went off."

"Look, this isn't getting us anywhere, "says Jenn. "Let's just move on."

All agreed and chatted a little."

"Come here and give me a hug, Paul."

"Okay, Tiffany."

As Paul leaned over, Tiffany takes his lighter out of his pocket without him knowing it.

"Hon, can I use your lighter?"

"Sure, wait... It's not here. I must've lost it running over here. Oh well. Hey, would you like to go out when you get off restriction?"

"Go out? What do you mean, Paul?"

"Umm... we are dating, did you forget?"

"Yeah, I guess I did, sorry!"

"It's okay a lot has happened. Would you go to dinner and a movie with me?"

"Yeah, sure."

"Well, I gotta go do my chores and then go to bed early."

"Okay, see you tomorrow."

"You and Paul are dating?"

"No. He wouldn't leave me alone, so I said yes to get him off my back. He says I remind him of this girl Marie he has a crush on back home."

"So, you're playing him?"

"I told him 100% I only want Jose. He won't leave me alone."

"It's okay. I'm just messing with you."

Tiffany and Jenn continued to chat on the porch and watched the sunset. Jenn went in to eat dinner and get ready for bed. The manipulator says to the Evil one.

"I told you I could get the job done."

"Don't pat yourself on the back yet, you are not done yet!"

"You worry too much, big guy. It will be a piece of cake."

"Just focus on getting the last piece done."

"I will."

Nighttime came. All slept peacefully. The girls were dreaming about the upcoming dance. What they would wear, who they would dance with. The guys didn't dream about the dance. They all dreamt about a variety of things. Jose dreamt of Jenn. He thought she was pretty. The other guys thoughts were all over the place. Girls, sports, music, food, cars, you name it. Tiffany's mind was clear of all thoughts. She woke up to her phone going off; it was Jose.

Wednesday, August 8, 1990

It is Wednesday, 3 days before the dance.

"Sorry to wake you, Tiff. We need to talk, can I come over?"

"Um...Well...I'm on restriction yet."

"Well it will only take a minute. If a staff member comes I will take full blame."

"I'm just getting up; can you give me an hour? Meet on the porch?"

"Alright see you then."

As Tiffany was getting ready for her talk with Jose, she thought to herself, *he wants me back. My man wants me back.* She put on her cute little black dress with the black heels that Jose loved to see her in. She put her hair up, put her makeup and his favorite perfume on. She couldn't wait to get Jose back. Jose. Couldn't wait to clear the air with Tiffany and to ask Jenn out on a date. It was 10:00, time for the meeting with Tiffany.

"Wow! Tiff, you look hot! "

"Thank you, Jose!"

"Look Tiff, I don't want to give you the wrong impression. This is not about us getting back together."

(Hurt and embarrassed), "Don't flatter yourself! I wore this for my new man. What did you want to talk about?"

"I'm still angry that you lied to me about everything. But, since we will be seeing each other a lot, I'm willing to drop it and move on."

"Sounds good to me! I just want to tell you how very sorry I am for hurting you the way I did. Can you forgive me?"

"Let's take things day by day. One more thing, is Jenn dating?"

"Jenn? I don't think so. Wait.... You came to get the scoop on Jenn? You picked her over me?"

"Let's not get into this. You and I are done. Nothing you say or do will change that. Can you give her my number?"

31

"Whatever! You are making a mistake! She's a whore! She will break your heart."

"Do this for me."

"FINE!"

"Thanks, Tiff."

Tiffany was both hurt and angry. Her tears stung her face as they streamed down her cheeks. Her heart was pounding like a drummer beating on a drum. She asked herself, *How could he do this to me? We will get even with her; she will pay with her life.*

Thought the Evil one.

Paul sees Tiffany on the porch and decides to stop over and say hi, on his way to the park.

"Hey sexy! Looking good! You're up early, normally you're just getting up. Did you dress sexy just to see me?"

She quickly dries her eyes, fixes herself, and says, "Yes, I did this all for my sweet pea.

How do I look? Do you like?"

"Yes, I like . You are hot! Why did you call me sweet pea?"

"It's my pet name for you. Do you like it?"

"Not really."

"What are your plans for today, Tiff?"

"Well I was hoping to show my man a good time."

"A good time? What does that mean?"

"You know? Having sex!"

(Blushing) "Ummm... well.... I'm still a.... Please don't laugh. I never had sex or dated before."

"OMG! You're a virgin? Really? Not even friends with benefits?

"What's friends with benefits?"

"Never mind. Look since this is your first time. Why don't we wait and plan something special?"

"Sounds good. I'm going for a walk. Talk to you later."

"Have fun on your walk."

"I will."

"What are your plans?"

"I can't do anything but sit here."

"Alright, see ya!"

On his walk, he couldn't stop fantasizing about making love to Tiffany. How he couldn't wait to feel her warm body close to him. To press his lips against her soft lips. *Well,* he thought, *only a few more days and she's off restriction. Then they can plan their big night together.* He was deep in thought when his phone began to ring. It was his stepdad, Sam.

"Great! What does nosey need to know now? Hey Sam, what's up?"

"Are you up for some company?"

"Well, I'm at the park, it will take me a few minutes to get back. Who all is with you?"

"Me, Scott, Joan and Marie. Joan had to take Marie to the ear doctor in Radner. We figured on visiting you since we will go right past there."

"How long will it take you to get here?" "About 20 minutes."

"Okay, I will wait on the porch for you."

"Alright, see you then."

Paul ran back to Pansy House. As he approached the house his family just pulled into the parking lot.

"Hey! Sam! Over here!"

"Hi, Marie, Scott, and Aunt Joan."

"Hey, how is it going?" Asked Scott.

"I'm good. Let's go inside. I'll show you around."

"Wow!" This is bigger than I thought."

"We can sit in the living room to chat. So, Marie, how's it going?"

"Ummm....good! The ear doctor said there's nothing they can do for my ears."

"Sorry to hear that."

"Thanks."

As they were talking, his roommate, Pete, comes in.

"Hey Pete! I want to introduce you to my family. This is my stepdad Sam, my Aunt Joan, my cousin Marie and my friend Scott."

"Are you the Marie dating Paul?"

"No! I am married. Paul wants me to date him. He has been stalking me."

"But you're cousins."

"We are not blood related. Besides, he is dating some girl named Tiffany."

"Tiffany!!! Why would you lic to us? "

"Look, can we discuss this after my family leaves, please Pete? "

"Yeah, I'm sorry. I didn't mean to offend anyone or start stuff. I just came in to play a game. It was nice meeting you all."

"No problem! We won't be long." Replies Sam.

"You're telling me you are dating Marie? What is the matter with you? Demands Aunt Joan.

"I just didn't want them knowing Tiff and I are dating. I didn't want to hear them cutting her down. I'll tell them it's Tiff. I'm sorry Marie."

" I forgive you this time. I am happily married to Brandon."

"I know! It won't happen again."

"Good." Says Aunt Joan. " When can we meet this Tiffany girl? Or, is she not even your girlfriend?"

"No Aunt Joan, we really are dating. She is on restriction right now for fighting with this girl named Jenn."

"Well, when she is off restriction, call and I will come back to meet her." "Okay. I will."

"So, Pete, where are you from? " asks Sam.

"I live not too far from you. I live in Limerick."

"Oh, where about?"

"If you go down Ridge Pike, when you get to the fire-house, there's a street just passed it on the right. Turn on the road and go about 3 blocks. We are in the huge brick house on the left."

"Okay. I know where you're at. You're past the trailer park."

"Yeah."

Scott says to Joan, "Sam can't go anywhere without him having to know where people are from or trucking stories. "

"At least he's not asking 50 million questions." Adds Paul.

"Are you doing your chores and whatever else they want you to do?"

"Yes, Aunt Joan, I do my chores and other peoples."

"Well that's nice of you."

"When you get home, can you let my dad know I owe my roommate 12 packs of ramen noodles?"

"Yes, I will. Well, Sam will beat me to it."

They stayed an hour and headed home. Sam just had to call Bob, Paul's dad. When Bob sees it's Sam, he rolls his eyes and says.

"Oh, great! Now what does he want? Hello!"

"I just wanted you to know that we were just at Paul's place to visit. Did you know that Paul's telling people he's dating Marie and that he owes his roommate 12 packs of ramen noodles?"

"Yes, Sam! I plan on bringing them up on Friday when I get paid."

"Does Paul know? Oh, I know what I wanted to tell you. I overheard someone saying that the girl he is dating was in prison."

"Yes, he knows. I'm not listening to your gossip. You are trying to get information on Tiffany. When you need to know something, Paul will tell you. Do you think Kym would like to come with me on Friday?"

"She isn't with us; you can call and ask her."

"Oh, Kym isn't with you?"

"No, just Scott, Joan and Marie. We had to bring Marie to Radnor to see the ear doctor." "Oh, how did it go?"

"It went alright. She was told there's nothing they can do for her. Then, do you want me to see if Kym wants to go with?"

"No, I'll give her a call. Hey, I have some things to take care of. Call you later?"

"Sure, no problem."

The ride home was nice and quiet, except for the other vehicles going by. Joan kept gazing at the scenery as they drove past. Sam called Kym to fill her in on his visit with Paul. Only giving her his version of the visit. Marie fell asleep on the way home.

After seeing Marie, Paul couldn't help daydreaming about Tiffany. He wishes their special night would be tonight. His thoughts were interrupted by a pissed off Pete.

"Why the hell did you lie to me about who you were dating?"

"Because we wanted to keep everything quiet for now."

"You made me look like an ass today. You could've pulled me aside and warned me. But instead you let me continue. I feel like a fool. "

"I'm sorry, I didn't know you would come down while they were here."

"Look, I don't care who you date. If you want to date the psych from next door, go for it. I expect you to be honest with me."

"You're right, I messed up. I'm sorry! Can we still be friends?"

"I'm just pissed that you lied to me. Be careful with Tiffany. I don't want to see you get hurt."

"Thanks for looking out for me. I hate to ask this, but can we keep who I am dating on the down low?"

"I won't lie to my friends. You need to figure this out with Tiffany."

"I get it!"

"I need to go. Catch you later, Paul."

Paul did his chores, ate dinner and went to bed. That night his thoughts were racing. He kept tossing for about an hour, so he gave up and just laid in bed, eyes wide open, and spent the night thinking about everything. His life, his girl, his messed up family. In the morning he started to drift off to sleep. As he was drifting to a deep sleep, his alarm went off. He jumped up!

THURSDAY. AUGUST 9, 1990

Thursday, 2 days before the dance.

He went to the bathroom slowly, slowly got dressed, slowly made his way downstairs to sit in the living room where Jose and Ralph were sitting. He sat on the couch, dozing off. Jose walks over to him.

"Hey, Paul, are you awake ?"

"Kinda, I didn't get any sleep last night."

"Daydreaming about your girl again?"

"Nah, thoughts racing in my mind. I just couldn't sleep."

"Would you like to jam with us?"

"Yeah! Thanks! Just let me go out, get some air and smoke a cigarette to wake up some."

"Alright, we practice in the basement."

"Okay."

Paul goes out for some air and sees Tiff on the porch. He decides to go chat for a bit.

"What's up, Tiff?"

"Not much. Since you are here, can I ask you a favor?"

"I guess so."

She pulls the plan out. Phase 1.

"Can you hide this in your room for me?"

"Where would I hide it though?"

"Under your bed."

"Yeah, I'll hide it."

"Thank you! Love you, sweet pea."

"I hate that name. Can you come up with a different name?"

"But I like that name."

"Okay. I need to head back. Jose invited me to jam with them."

"They can't practice without me! I'm the lead singer! I'm giving him a call."

"Calm down, Tiffany."

"Do you understand that I'm the lead? I made the band. Without me that band is nothing! The people come to see the lead singer, not everyone else."

"Alright I get it!"

"Jose, question, did you call a practice without me?"

"I can call a practice anytime I want to. I don't have to include you."

"If it wasn't for me, there would be no band. I made you all."

"Get over yourself! You think too highly of yourself. The band was here before you and me. It was started by a staff member."

"Why would you call a practice with me on restriction?"

"Did you forget we were playing songs at the dance Saturday?"

"Yeah, I did. And since I'm on restriction, you still need to practice."

"Now you get it?"

"I'm sorry."

"Now can I go get ready for band?"

"Alright, bye. Paul, you better get going, they are getting ready to start."

"Are you sure? I don't mind staying with you

"No, I'd rather you go. This way you can be like a spy for me."

"A spy?"

"Yeah, tell me if they vote me out and who replaces me. What songs they are doing at the dance. Can you do that for me?"

"Yes!"

Paul gives her a kiss on the cheek, goes to the house and down the basement where band practice is. Tiffany continues sitting on the porch. Leaning back in her chair. The light breeze breathing through her hair. The sun, shining on her face. Just her and her thoughts. The manipulator says to the evil one.

"I told you I could pull it off."

"It's not a success until every part of the plan is executed."

" You watch, everything will go as planned."

"It better! Or you will pay!"

"Hey, Paul! Glad you came." Says Jose.

"Sorry about Tiff."

"It's alright, don't sweat it. She would've found out anyway. Besides, it's better to argue with her before practice and not during."

"Alright guys, gather around, we have a few things to discuss." Says Terry, the in charge staff member."

"First, Jose, in spite of what has happened between you and Tiffany, are you going to be okay with her being the lead singer?"

"It's all good, Terry. I'm okay with it. Her voice is how we are known, not just our sound."

"Good point! Second, how about making Paul a band member? Do you play any instruments?"

"I play a little guitar, I'm not that good."

"Well, between me and Ralph helping you, you will be playing in no time. Ain't that right,

Ralph?"

"Yep!"

" Thanks?"

"No problem. Me and the guys are glad to have you in our band. Now! Does anyone have any suggestions as to what to play at the dance?"

Why don't we take a list of songs we all know and have them pick the songs when they enter. When the DJ is playing, we tally them up and play the ones most picked." Suggests Pete.

"That sounds good, but we know so many songs it will take awhile. Why don't we pick 6 songs and have them pick 3? We are only playing 3 songs anyway." Added Ralph.

"Both ideas are good. It's up to you Jose. Whose idea should we go with?"

"I like Ralph's, shouldn't our new member get to vote?"

"I think we should go with Ralph's."

"Ralph's it is. I want Pete and Paul to team up and pick 6 songs. And the same for Jose and Ralph. Then we will take a private vote . The most votes win."

It took an hour for the teams to pick 6 songs. Then a half hour to tally up. The songs they choose: I will always love you, Whoop! (There it is), Poison, Baby got back, Hero, and How do I know.

After agreeing on the 6 they began to practice until 8:00 p.m. then they were off to bed. Paul was excited about being in the band. Since he didn't sleep well last night. When his head hit the pillow, he fell fast asleep. He had a peaceful sleep.

FRIDAY, AUGUST 10,1990

Morning time! It's Friday, 1day before the dance. Both girls and guys were at the social hall setting up for the big night. Decorations went up. The stage was being set up for the band. The platform is ready for the DJ. Tables were set up for the food, beverages , and everyone to sit at.

The evil one is all set to go. Tiffany, Jenn, and Paul all sat on the porch chatting. Neither one helped to set up since they couldn't attend the dance. Tiffany and Jenn were talking like nothing happened. The three of them enjoyed each other's company.

"Paul, tell me what happened during band practice."

"I'm in the band now, they voted me in. Terry started by asking Jose if he is okay with you being the lead singer still, despite everything that's happened between you both.

What did he mean by that?"

"Don't worry about it. It's a long story. Has anything else happened?"

" Terry and Ralph said they would teach me guitar. We choose 6 songs and out of those 6, each boy and girl will pick 3 songs. They will be tallied up and the 3 with the most votes get played."

"Thanks, sweet pea. Hey Jenn, do you have a boyfriend?"

"Why do you want to know?"

"I don't want to know, Jose asked me."

"Really! He did? Tell him no for me."

"Okay, would you like his number?"

"Yes, please."

"It's 555-932-2232, give him a call or text."

"I know how much you like Jose. Are you sure you're okay with me and Jose dating?"

"Well, I have to be. I messed up. Besides, I'm with someone else now."

"Thank you Tiff."

"Hey Tiff, what are you doing during the dance?" Asks Paul.

I'm watching some movies in my room. Just to relax. How about you, Jenn?"

"I'm spending most of the time at the park. I will be there until 7 then come home and rest on my comfy bed. What about you, Paul?"

"I'm spending the day with my mom and dad."

"Where are you from?"

"I'm from Pottstown. Where are you from, Jenn?"

"I'm from Perkiomenville."

"My aunt has a friend who lives there."

"Do you know where about?"

"Up by the S.P.C.A"

"I live past the nursing home."

"Okay."

"Hey," says Jenn, "Do you want to play cards?"

"What game?"

"Rummy."

"Count us in."

They played cards, chatted for a while, cracked jokes all the way up to curfew. Then they went to bed. The evil one says to Tiffany, "After tomorrow, no more Jenn." Paul will get arrested for the murder. And with them gone, never to return, Jose would be Tiffany s, or so she thought.

Saturday, August 11,1990

The day everyone was waiting for has finally arrived! The girls were getting their hair and nails done. Some were getting last minute alterations on their dresses and last minute accessories. Tiffany had her movies and plan ready to go. Jenn packed some drinks and food to have a picnic at the park. Paul couldn't wait to see his parents. The band was practicing the songs they picked. The DJ was setting up his equipment. The food and beverages were arriving. The girls decorated all the tables with red and white carnations in the center with small tea candles. The theme of the dance is summer romance. They had hearts with cupids hanging from the ceiling. It was almost time for the dance to start, both sides wondered who they would be dancing with. Jose wished Jenn was going. Everything was going according to plan. No one had a clue that tonight would end in tragedy.

Before the dance began, Juniper came to go over the song selection for the band and what they can and can't do. The rules were as follows.

1. No alcohol! If caught you will be kicked out of the dance and kicked out of Pansy House.
2. No dirty dancing allowed. If caught both parties will be kicked out of Pansy House.

We want you all to have a good time. Once the doors were opened, the DJ started playing. They all picked the songs they wanted the band to play. Paul went with his parents to the mall.

"Hey, buddy! Where would you like to eat?"

"Dad, I'm not a kid anymore. Let's go to a Chinese place."

"Do we get to meet this girlfriend of yours?"

No, mom, Tiffany is on restriction for fighting this girl"

" I was on the phone with Sam that day. He was here to visit you. He said Tiffany was in jail."

" Dad, you know how Sam is. He has to cause trouble and is always trying to get information. I don't know if she's ever been in jail. I know her and Jenn had to go to the police station to give a statement. That's all!"

"Hey, let's enjoy our time together."

"Dad, I know you are only concerned about me. But I'm fine. And Mom is right, let's enjoy shopping."

"Well shopping it is."

Back at Pansy House, Tiffany and Jenn were getting ready to do what they planned.

And the dance had already started.

"So, Jenn, are you getting ready to leave?"

"Yes, I will be back at 8:00 p.m."

" I'm relaxing in my room watching movies."

"Cool, I will see you later."

Tiffany went into her room for the night. Time for the evil one to take over. He waited an hour after Jenn left. Then he slowly crept into Jenn's room and started to loosen the bolts around the base of the ceiling fan. Just enough to where when Jenn turns the fan on it will kill her on impact. Then waited for Jenn to return. And have the lighter taken from Paul ready to plant.

Between the band and the DJ, the music was so loud that if a person was screaming, no one would hear them. The evil one hid in Jenn's roommates closet, that way as soon as Jenn is dead, the lighter will get put in Jenn's hand. Paul had a good visit with his parents, he hated to see them go. Jenn started her way back home. She loved it at the park. It was so, peaceful, no fighting, no arguing. Just beautiful, chirping of the birds. Oh well, another day perhaps.

Paul had gone to bed early, despite the loud music from the dance. The dance wouldn't be over till 11:00. Plenty of time for the murder to be done. Jenn came in, grabbed a snack, took a shower, laid on her bed, and pulled the long cord to turn on the ceiling fan. Before she could even move, the ceiling fan came down spinning on top of her. She didn't even have time to scream. Jenn's guts and blood went everywhere. Her body lay there like an empty shell. All that was left of her body was her legs and the spine of her back, still attached to her hips. She no longer had a head, chest, stomach, or organs. The evil one waited a few moments, then tiptoed on the only floor space not covered by blood or guts. He carefully and slowly placed the lighter on what was left of her body. This way Paul would get blamed for Jenn's death, Tiffany and Jose would be reunited again.

A couple of hours went by, kids started leaving the dance. They all had an excellent time. When Jenn's roommate, Sue came back, she walks in the room and starts screaming and yelling.

"HELP! SOMEONE PLEASE! HELP ME! MY ROOMMATE IS..."

She couldn't finish due to the heaviness of her tears and she was vomiting from the blood and guts. Tiffany was first to arrive. She saw the blood and guts and vomited in the hallway. Then she called 911.

"911, what's your emergency?"

"HELP US! PLEASE! Our friend, she's dead! A sobbing Tiffany says.

"Calm down, ma'am. Tell me what happened."

Crying, Tiffany says, " I live at Pansy House, girls dorm #1. Something happened to my friend. She's dead!"

"Okay, ma'am someone will be there shortly. Please stay on the phone until someone arrives."

"Alright."

Homicide detectives were first to arrive. Followed by the coroner, the crime unit, ambulance, and more police. Sue and Tiffany were shaking and crying. After seeing the crime scene, the detectives went to talk to the girls. Detective Deets talks to Tiffany, and Detective Berks talks to Sue.

Flashing badges, "We are Detectives Deets and Berks from homicide. Let's start with your names and how you know the victim?"

"My name is Tiffany Powers, I'm just a friend."

"My name is Sue Cox, I'm, well, was, Jenn Crumb's roommate."

"Miss Powers, why don't we come over here to discuss what happened, and Miss Cox can go with Detective Berks"

"All I know is Sue came back from the dance about 11ish went to her room and (crying) she saw Jenn all over the room. I came when she screamed. I called 911."

"Out of everyone here, only you heard Miss Cox scream?"

"Some were at the co-ed dance held in the social hall. I was the first to come. My room is down the hall."

"Were you at the dance? Did anyone have a dispute with Miss Crumbs?"

"Jenn and I weren't at the dance. Me, Jenn, and Paul were on restriction and couldn't go to the dance."

"Where were you at about 8:30-9:30 p.m.?"

"Well, I stayed in and watched movies. I had the tv up loud to hear because the music from the dance was loud. I couldn't hear."

"Did you see or hear anything suspicious or out of the ordinary?"

"No!"

"Did you see anyone who didn't belong here?"

"No!"

"Did anyone have issues with Miss Crumbs, hold any-thing against her, hate her?"

"No! Everyone loved her."

"Okay, that is all for now. Don't go anywhere. I may have more questions."

"Miss Cox, can you tell me what happened?"

(crying and shaking) "I was at the dance until 11 p.m. I opened the door and saw Jenn, everywhere. As I was screaming, Tiff came running, she threw up in the hallway and called 911."

"Did you hear or see anything out of the ordinary? Did you see anyone who didn't belong?"

"The music was loud. I couldn't hear much. I didn't see anything or anyone out of the ordinary."

"Do you know of anyone who had any problems with Miss Crumb, or may have wanted her dead?"

"Not that I can think of. Wait…about a week ago, Jenn and Tiffany got into a huge fight. Tiff got pushed down the steps and she lost the baby. That same night, Tiffany's boyfriend left her."

"What is the boyfriend's name?"

"Jose Nightwolf, he lives in boys #1."

"Okay, thank you. That's all for now. Don't go anywhere, I may have more questions." "Okay."

The detectives head back to the crime scene to see what the coroner, Doc Matthews, could tell them.

"Hey, Doc Matthews, can you tell me the time of death?"

"Well, she died on impact. I doubt she felt any pain. I put the time of death between 8:30 and 9:30 p.m. In all my 30 years of doing this job, I have never seen anything this disturbing."

"Neither have we, Doc, neither have we. Let's see if the crime unit has anything."

" Hey, Joe! What do you have for us?"

"Hey, Detective Deets. Well there wasn't much with her guys and blood everywhere. But we found this lighter on her pillow. We are still going through stuff."

"Well, just do the best you can. What did you learn from the Cox girl?"

"I learned something interesting. About a week ago, Miss Powers had an altercation with our victim. Miss Crumb and Miss Powers got into a fight. Miss Powers got pushed down the stairs, she lost her baby, and her boyfriend dumped her. Other than that, Miss Cox left the dance at 11 p.m., went into her room, and found our victim everywhere. Miss

Powers came when she heard Miss Cox screaming. Miss Powers got sick in the hallway and called 911. What about you?"

" Nothing really, just what you told me, except, she forgot to mention the altercation between her and Miss Crumb, not even that she lost her baby and boyfriend all in the same day."

Crime scene tape was put up to barricade the door and a female cop was seated at the door so no one would bother the crime scene. All the commotion sparked the curiosity of the staff and the rest of the kids at the dance. Juniper walked over to Detective Deets to get some answers.

"Can I help you ma'am?"

"Yes, I am Juniper Kincade, the director here at Pansy House. Can you tell me what is going on her"

"I'm Detective Deets, one of the Detectives on this case. One of your girls in dorm #1,

Miss Crumb, is no longer with us."

"What? What do you mean? Someone killed her? OMG!"

"Ms. Kincade, we don't have all the facts as to what happened. All I can say for sure is there has been a horrible crime committed, and a person is dead. When I know more, I will let you know. Can I ask you a few questions?"

"Umm.. Sure."

"What can you tell me about the altercation between Miss a and Miss Powers?"

"Well.... A fight broke out between Jenn and Tiffany over Tiffany talking badly about

Jenn. Jenn was only trying to push Tiffany away and she fell down the stairs. When Jose saw Jenn at the police station, he wanted Jenn arrested for Tiffany losing the baby, which it turned out, that Tiffany was never pregnant."

"So, Mr. Nightwolf had an altercation with her too. Have you seen this lighter before?" "No!"

"Can you give me the contact information for Miss Crumb's parents?"

"Sure, follow me to my office."

At the crime scene, forensics figured out how the fan fell. Detective Berks started asking the boys and girls questions. All were in a state of confusion. They couldn't believe that a friend of theirs was dead. Was she murdered? If so, who is next?

"Hey, Detective Berks!"

"What's up, Joe? Have you gotten anything else from the victims room?"

"We figured out how the fan fell. It looks like someone loosened the bolts just enough so that it would only fall when the cord was pulled. Once the cord was pulled, the fan starts spinning. The spinning of the fan loosened the bolts more and the fan fell. There were no fingerprints, whoever did this was very thorough. The fan was still spinning when it fell. Just by the way her guys and blood were splattered all over like a fan effect."

"Well done. Thanks, Joe."

"Excuse me, can you point me to a Jose Nightwolf?"

"He is not here. Can I help you?"

"I am Detective Berks, can you tell me how you know Miss Crumb"

"I am Ralph Parker, I stay in boys dorm #1. Jenn and I are just friends."

"Do you know of anyone who would want to hurt Jenn?"

"Tiffany Powers. The girls got into a fight and we're put on restriction a week ago. Tiffany was pissed about it. One thing you should know, Tiff gets even with anyone who crosses her."

"Thank you! Is there anyone else I should speak to?"

"Maybe Jose. He got a pass to stay at a friend's place."

"Give him my card and have him call me A.S.A.P."

"Sure."

"Here it is! Her parent's names are Billy and Kathy Crumb. They live at 6787 Little Rd.

Perkiomenville. The phone number is 613-670-8270."

"Thank you! Can you think of anyone who would want to hurt Miss Crumb?"

"Well, last week Jenn and Paul Montgomery had a misunderstanding. I don't know all the details except Tiffany Powers was involved. Paul was very angry with Jenn.

Something about Jenn choking Tiffany."

"Tiffany's name is coming up a lot. Where can I find Mr. Montgomery?"

"He had a visit with his parents today. I don't know if he came back yet."

"Here is my card. Have him contact me right away."

"I have a question. Jenn's roommate will need to get her clothes and stuff."

"I will have someone get what they can. It will take a few weeks to get that room cleaned."

"I have another room to put her in."

The coroner took what was left of Jenn's body and guts. The Detectives got enough information to start with. Sue was put into Tiffany's room permanently.

The evil one was proud of himself. Everything went according to plan. All that's needed is for Paul to be arrested for the murder. The excitement of Tiffany's first murder was a feeling she hadn't felt in a long time. She was cool, calm, and confident. A sense of peace came upon her. She felt invincible! No one would ever know it was Tiffany Powers.

No one slept that night. They no longer felt safe. The thought of a stranger or someone amongst them being able to pull off a murder right under their noses was a haunting thought. Who would be next among them, if any? Would they ever catch who did this?

SUNDAY, AUGUST 12, 1990

It was the next morning, the Detectives were already heading to Jenn's parent's.

Telling them their daughter was murdered was one thing. What if they ask how or want to see her? That is something neither Berks or Deets were ready to deal with.

"Good morning, ma'am, we are looking for Mr and Mrs Crumb."

"I am Mrs Crumb, how can I help you?"

"My name is Detective Deets, this is my partner Detective Berks. Can we come in?"

" Sure, let me get my husband."

"We are sorry to bother you this early in the morning. Sorry to have to tell you this. Your daughter Jenn has been murdered."

Mrs Crumb fell to her knees crying. "NOOOOOOO! NOT MY JENNIE! PLEASE TELL

ME IT ISN'T SO?"

Mr Crumb stood there in shock, speechless, as the tears stung his face, streaming down his cheek.

I'm sorry, ma'am. She was murdered between 8:30-9:30 p.m. last night. I know this is a difficult time but, do either of you know if she had any enemies or people who would want to hurt her?"

"No one wanted to hurt Jennie, everyone got along with her. She was popular." Says Mr Crumb.

"Do you have any leads, Detectives?"

"Yes, we do. There are 3 people we are looking into, Tiffany Powers, Paul Montgomery and a Jose Nightwolf. They recently had altercations with Jenn." "When will we have her body to bury her?" Asks Mrs Crumb.

"Well, there is not much left of her to bury."

"What do you mean, Detective? How did Jenn die?" Mr Crumb demanded.

"A ceiling fan fell on her. It hit her so fast, she felt no pain. Before I tell you this next part, can I ask Mrs Crumb to leave the room? This part is graphic."

"I'm not leaving, what you say to my husband you can say to me. I can take it."

"If you insist. The fan was still spinning when it hit her. All that's left of her are legs, hips and backbone. Her blood and guts were everywhere."

Her mother ran out of the room, sick to her stomach. She ran outside vomiting. Her husband sat down sobbing with his head in his hands." "My little girl."

"Who would do such a thing? She was a kind sweet girl." Sobbed the Crumbs.

"We are working hard to find out who did this. We have 3 people of interest. I am confident her killer will be caught. Here are our cards. Feel free to call us night or day.

Again, we are sorry for your loss."

"Thank you Detectives."

Neither one spoke a word on the way back to Bryn Mawr. It was quiet; you could hear a pin drop. Not even traffic disturbed the quietness. Having to tell the Crumbs how their only child was murdered was worse than seeing what was left with their own eyes. Detective Deets thought of his own children and how he would feel if any of them were murdered like the Crumb girl. Detective Berks thought of his unborn child, his only child, would his pain be as severe as what the Crumbs are going through? When they got back to the station, Jose was there to see them.

"Detectives, a Jose Nightwolf is here to see you."

"Thank you, officer."

"Mr Nightwolf, I'm Detective Deets, and this is my partner Detective Berks. Follow us, we will get straight to the reason you are here."

"How well did you know Jenn Crumb?" Asked Detective Berks.

"She and I are friends. I don't know her that well. Why?"

"She was found dead last night by her roommate, Sue. Where were you between 8:30 p.m. and 9:30 p.m. last night?"

(Crying, Jose says), " I was at the dance, then I spent the night at a friend's house. I got there around 10:00 p.m."

"Will your friend verify you were there?"

"Yes, her name is Denise, her number is 610-555-3269."

"We will check your alibi, if it checks out you're free to go."

Jose sat at the police station crying over the death of his friend Jenn, whom he was hoping to date as Detective Berks checked his alibi.

"Hello!"

"Can I speak to Denise?"

"This is her."

"My name is Detective Berks from Bryn Mawr homicide. I am investigating a murder that happened at Pansy House. Can you tell me if Jose Nightwolf was with you last night?"

"Yes, he was."

"What time did he arrive?"

"About 10:00 p.m."

"Okay, thank you."

(Turning to Detective Deets)

"Well, his alibi checks out."

"Ok, I have just one more question to ask him."

"Alright, let's go in."

"Mr. Nightwolf, could you tell me about the altercation between you and Miss Crumb's about 2 weeks ago?"

" There was a fight between her and my fiancé at the time, Tiffany. Tiffany went down the stairs. Supposedly Tiffany lost our baby. I was hurt and angry when I saw her at the police station. I went off! Then Officer Menendez showed me the doctor's report that proved Tiffany wasn't ever pregnant. I apologized to Jenn. That's all that was to it."

"Have you ever seen this lighter before?"

"It looks like the new kid's, Paul Montgomery."

"Your alibi checks out, you're free to go. Don't leave town, we may have more questions."

"Okay."

Jose left the station crying. His thoughts began to race. How he wasted time dating Tiffany. How he never got the chance to tell Jenn how he truly felt about her.

At Pansy House, almost everyone was still in shock from last night. Tiffany woke up refreshed, ready to go. Sue didn't sleep at all. Her mind was horrified over the sight of her friend. Who could do such a thing to a sweet, compassionate girl like Jenn? She would miss her smile and laugh. The smell of her perfume which made the room smell like roses. She would miss how they stayed up late talking the night away.

Sue was exhausted, her eyes wanted to close but couldn't. Juniper came in to see how she was doing.

"Sue, how are you doing today?"

"I am not doing well. I didn't sleep last night. Every time I close my eyes, the images of

Jenn haunt me."

"It will take time for your mind to refocus on something positive, especially after what just happened. We are all here for you if you need to talk."

"Thank you. Would it be okay if I go home for a little to clear my mind?"

"Let's call your parents and see what they say about it."

"Can we call now?"

"Sure, come to my office."

As they headed to Juniper's office, memories of Jenn kept flashing in Sue's mind. She couldn't handle the pain she felt inside her. By the time she got to Juniper's office, Sue was sobbing.

"Hello!"

"Hey, mom, it's me Sue."

"Are you alright?"

"Well, no. Something horrible happened last night and I wondered if I could come home for a little while?'

"Is Juniper close by? I want to speak to her."

"Here she is."

"Juniper, what is going on? Why does she really want to leave?"

"Last night during the dance, Sue's roommate, Jenn, was brutally murdered in their room. Sue found her remains. I think some time from here would be in Sue's best interest. We can hold her spot for 6 months."

"Oh dear. Tell her to pack some stuff, her dad and I will be up today. I am scheduling therapy right away. If more time is needed can she get it?"

"In a case like this, we will work something out."

"Thank you!"

"Sue, your mom said to pack your stuff they will be here tonight to get you."

"Ok, thanks Juniper."

"You're welcome."

The guys were sitting on the porch when Jose approached, dazed and confused. He couldn't stop thinking about the events that took place last night. He felt guilty for going to the dance. He should've been there to protect Jenn. Little did he know, there was nothing he could've done to protect her from the evil lurking in Pansy House. If she didn't die this time, she would've died next time. His thoughts were interrupted by Paul.

"Hey! How's it going Jose?"

"Get your damn hands off me, Paul."

"Yo, what's wrong? What did I do to you"

"YOU KNOW DAMN WELL WHAT YOU DID TO JENN! ADMIT IT!"

"Ummm.... What happened to Jenn?"

"YOU KILLED HER!"

"I have no clue what you are talking about."

"The police have proof. They found your lighter at the scene."

"Can someone please tell me what the hell is going on?"

"Don't act like you don't know."

"ENOUGH!" shouted Pete. "Maybe he honestly doesn't know. Look, sometime last night, during the dance, Jenn was brutally murdered in her room."

"Murdered? When? How? Who?"

"Her fan fell on her when she turned it on. Sue found her when she went back to her room. Her guys and blood were everywhere."

"And..." added Jose. "They found your lighter on her pillow."

"You think I killed her? I got back from my parents at 8:00 p.m. then I went to bed. I didn't hear a sound."

"Come to think of it." Says Pete, "when I came in at about 9 p.m. he was fast asleep. He didn't even budge."

"Fine! Whatever! So, he didn't do it. Then who did ?" Asked Jose.

"Hey, does anyone know how Sue is doing?" Asked Paul.

"We were hoping to see Juniper to ask her. Here she comes."

"Hi boys. How are you doing?"

"We are all doing good. We all are wondering how Sue is doing?" Asked Pete.

"She isn't doing too well. She is going home for a few months. I'm glad I ran into you

Paul. Detective Deets would like you to stop in. He has some questions to ask you."

"Can someone take me? I don't know where it is."

"Come on, I will take you."

"Thank you, Juniper."

Neither one said a word on the way to the police station. Juniper was deep in thought about how to change security, programs and rules. All to better the quality of life at Pansy House. Paul was nervous about going to the police station. What would they ask him? How did they get his lighter? He lost it a week ago. How will this affect his relationships with his new friends? Then he changed his thoughts to Tiffany. Did she get hurt last night? They pulled into a large parking lot with a brick building. There were police cars parked along the left side of the building. He went in and asked to speak with Detective Deets.

"Can I speak to Detective Deets?"

"Sure, one moment."

"Detective Deets, someone is here to see you."

"I will be right there."

"I'm Detective Deets, how can I help you?"

"I'm Paul Montgomery from Pansy House. I was told you wanted to speak with me."

"Oh yes, follow me and have a seat in there. I will be right back."

"Alright, Mr Montgomery, where were you between 8:30-9:30 p.m. last night?"

"I got back from my parents at about 8:00 p.m. I went to bed shortly after that."

"Would your parents verify you were with them?"

"Yeah. My dad's name is Bob Montgomery, 304-555-8964

My mom's name is Kym Plumber, 304-555-6080."

"Do you recognize this lighter?"

"It's mine. I lost it a week ago. Where did you find it?"

"It was found next to what was left of Jenn Crumb. If you didn't put it there, who did?"

"I don't know. I haven't seen that lighter in a week. I lent it to Tiffany and haven't seen it since."

"Tiffany Powers? She never gave it back?"

"Yes, Tiffany borrowed it. I thought she gave it back. I couldn't find it so I figured I lost it."

"Ok. Wait here, we need to check your alibi, and a few things out. Detective Berks, can you call Kym Plumber, check his alibi and I will call his dad."

"No problem."

"Hello!"

"Can I speak to Kym Plumber?"

"This is her."

"My name is Detective Berks from Bryn Mawr homicide. Paul Montgomery said he was with you until 8 p.m. last night. Can you verify that?"

"Umm... yeah! He was with me and his dad. We picked him up at lunch time. We were gone the whole day."

"And who are you to Paul?"

"I am his mother."

"Thank you! You've been very helpful."

"Hello!"

"I am looking for Bob Montgomery."

"This is Bob

"I am Detective Deets from Bryn Mawr Homicide Unit. Your son Paul claims he was with you till about 8 P.M. last night.Is this true?"

"We got him at 12 pm and dropped him off at about 8 P.M.Why do you need to know his wear abouts?"

"A girl was murdered last night at Pansy House. We are checking on everyone who was not at the dance at that hour.Thank you and have a nice day."

"Detective Berks, did everything check out?"

"Yes, all is good on my end. What about you?"

"He was gone from 12 P.M. -8 P.M. I need to check one more thing, then I will be in."

"Forensics, Tom speaking."

"This is Detective Deets, can I speak with Joe?"

"Sure, hey Joe, Deets is on the phone for you."

"Deets, what can I do for you?"

"I was wondering if there were any other fingerprints on the lighter, other than the victim's?"

"I haven't found any. If I come up with anything new, you will be the first to know."

"Thanks ,Joe."

"Well?" asks Detective Berks.

"Nope!"

"Nothing new. Let me send Mr. Montgomery on his way."

"Well, Mr. Montgomery, your alibi checks out. I have one more question to ask you. Can you tell me about the altercation between you and Miss Crumb?"

"I got a text from Tiff saying that she needed help, Jenn was hurting her. I rushed over and it looked like Jenn was choking Tiffany. I was yelling at Jenn to get off Tiffany. It turned out Jenn and Tiffany were apologizing for the big fight they had, Jenn was only hugging Tiff."

"So, let me get this straight Tiffany told you Jenn was hurting her, when she was giving her a hug?"

"Yes!"

"Can you please tell Miss. Powers to come down to the station? I have more questions for her."

"Sure."

Back at Pansy House, Juniper had grief and trauma therapists on standby if anyone needed to talk. Some of the kids needed someone to talk to. Others made fun of them, but deep down they were struggling with what happened. Tiffany was one who laughed. The liar personality within her decided to have some fun with the therapist.

"Hello, my name is Janet, how can I help you?"

"Well I need to get my feelings out. Can I talk to you?"

"Sure, why don't you give me your name?"

"My name is Chrissy."

"Let's start with how well you knew Jenn Crumb?"

"We were very close, closer than her roommate, Sue."

"Oh, okay! First, I want to reassure you that there may or may not have been any way to prevent what happened. Now that that's out of the way, tell me what's on your mind. I don't know what to do with Jenn gone. She was my only friend. You have no other friends to socialize with?"

"Not really. Sometimes I chat with Tiffany."

"I want you to try and interact with at least one other person. Well, our time is up.

Let's reschedule for Monday at noon."

"Is that all? I haven't been here long."

"I'm sorry, I have so many people to see. I can only see each one for 45 minutes."

"Okay, I get it. Monday at noon is good."

No one slept that night, except Tiffany.

MONDAY, AUGUST 13, 1990

Everyone was still in shock about the new rule. No one liked it, but they know there is nothing they can do about it. The evil one was furious with the liar for starting something he has to finish. So, the evil one told the liar exactly what to do to take care of the problem she created. That she needs to reschedule the appointment to where she is the last one seen. The acid was ready to go. The person before the liar had just left. Jose didn't recognize Chrissy. Now to put the plan into action. The acid she would be pouring into Janet's tea was fast acting acid. It would take effect throughout the night, by morning, no more Janet.

"Okay, Chrissy, go in and sit down. I will be right back."

Chrissy quickly grabbed Janet's tea, emptied all the acid into it. Stirred it and put it back where Janet had it.

"Hey, how come there is no one with you?"

"I told you I have no friends. Plus, I can walk by myself."

"I didn't mean anything by it. Just that there was a meeting by Juniper that no one can walk anywhere alone from 5 P.M.-7 A.M."

"Oh, I wasn't here this weekend, I didn't know."

"I need to ask you a question, Chrissy. Do you know the person who was ahead of you?"

"Nope, never seen him before."

"That's interesting since he resides at Pansy House and was one of Jenn's friends. He never heard of you either. In fact, no one has, not even staff."

"Well, they wouldn't. I'm new here."

"Juniper doesn't even know you. She claims the only new person in the last month is a boy named Paul Montgomery."

"Okay, the truth is, I'm homeless and Jenn would allow me to take a shower, she fed me and did my wash. We did get close. No one knew."

"Why didn't you tell me that?"

"Because I was afraid of being arrested."

"Where are you going now?"

"To the lake."

"You can come to my place. I'm in room 214 at the hotel next door."

"Thank you!'

"Well, I'm getting thirsty, would you like some tea?"

"I'm good."

"That's all for today. Stop by at 7:00."

"Okay, thanks."

"See you then."

Janet poured herself a glass of tea. She tripped on the rug. The glass of tea spilled all over her chest and stomach area. The acid started working immediately. Janet felt her skin burning like she was on fire. She splashed some cold water on herself. But it made it worse. Her flesh was burned up even quicker. She tried to scream, no one could hear her. By the time her flesh was gone, all that was left was her head, bones, and her organs, which still worked. Janet was still alive! Her remaining parts just laid there. In her mind all she could think about was someone coming to put her out of her misery. No one came for 2 days. She had no appointments; the secretary was on vacation. She couldn't speak, couldn't feel. She didn't even have tears to cry.

THURSDAY, AUGUST 16,1990

It was a warm Thursday morning. Everyone was starting to deal with the murder of

Jenn and the fact that the killer was still out there! A sense of fear was starting to settle upon Pansy House. No one could possibly be prepared for the terror that awaits them.

Juniper was getting worried about Janet. She hadn't heard from her in a couple of days. The office was quiet, an unsettling feeling came over her. As she slowly opened the therapist's door, a horrible odor came through the opening crack. When she fully opened the door, terror came across her. Her body froze, she couldn't move. She tried to cry for help but couldn't get the words out. Tears ran down her face like heavy rainfall in April. She stood there for 15 minutes, but to her it seemed like hours. She was all alone with what was left of Janet. Nothing but a head and organs. Juniper was startled by what sounded like a small drum beating. She leaned in to see where the sound was coming from. There amongst Janet's organs was her heart beating, weakly.

"That's odd, a heart stops beating when you're dead." She thought to herself.

She looked at Janet's head and saw her lips move some, and her eyes twitched.

"OMG!" she said aloud " SHE'S ALIVE!" Juniper quickly dialed 911.

"911,what is your emergency?"

"My friend is barely alive, come help quick!"

"Slow down, ma'am, and tell me what is wrong."

"I walked into my friend's office and only saw her organs and head, but she is

still alive."

"Okay, ma'am, this is an emergency number for people who have a real emergency. Your prank call may have ended someone's life. Call back when there's a real emergency."

"NO, WAIT! DON'T HANG UP! I'M TELLING THE TRUTH! PLEASE BELIEVE ME."

"Okay, ma'am, this is what I will do. I will send the paramedics and police. Give me your name and address. I warn you though, if this is a prank, not only will you be heavily fined, you will also be in jail for 30-120 days!"

"I understand. My name is Juniper Kincade, I'm at Pansy House, I'm in building D. Come quickly, she's very weak."

"Police and paramedics are on their way. Please stay on the line until one of them shows up."

"Okay, the police are here."

Juniper went out to meet the police. As Juniper took Officer Carl to Jane's office, the residents and staff started to gather around to see what's going on. The police put barricades up to keep everyone back. Officer Carl carelessly walked over to where Janet's remains lay, trying to tape off the area before someone stepped on her organs. He took a step back and stepped right on her heart, killing Janet accidently. He now became part of the crime scene. The paramedics came to examine the remains. Relief came over Officer Carl when he heard she would've been dead in a few hours anyway. Officer Carl was given slippers so he could take off his shoes and leave them at the crime scene. The coroner arrived to take the remains to the morgue. He told Officer Carl to call Detective Deets in homicide."

"Homicide! Detective Deets, how can I help you?"

"This is Officer Carl, I am at Pansy House building D, we have another homicide."

"Detective Deets and I will be right over. Berks, we have another murder at Pansy House."

"Okay, let's go."

It took them 15 minutes to get there. As Detective Deets walked past the crowds, standing at the barricade is Tiffany and Paul with a big grin on their faces. They got to the crime scene and caught a glimpse of Janet's remains before the coroner closed the body bag. They couldn't believe what they saw. Officer Carl was the first to approach the detectives.

"Before you begin, I need to tell you up front that as I was taping off the area, I accidently stepped on her heart."

"Thank you for being honest with us. Now where can we find Juniper Kincade?"

"She is right over there."

"Ms. Kincade, can we ask you a few questions?"

"Sure, Detective Deets. What would you like to know?"

"Well, can you tell me how long she's been like this?"

"I don't know. I got concerned when I didn't hear from her in a few days. I found her like this when I got here."

"Did you hear or see anything out of the ordinary or see someone that doesn't belong?"

"No, just that I haven't heard from her in a few days."

"Do you know who she saw last?"

"No, but I can look through her calendar."

"Wait until forensics goes through everything and gets fingerprints, "says Detective Deets.

"Okay, this is the second murder in a few weeks, do you think they are connected?" asks Detective Berks.

"I can't say for certain, but if I had to guess, I would say that due to the gruesomeness of both murders, I would say yes, they may be connected."

"Detective Deets!"

"Yes Joe, did you find anything?"

"Well her last appointment was with a girl named Chrissy."

"Chrissy? Are you sure?"

"Yes, she was seen at 2:00 on Monday."

"Okay, thank you, Joe. Juniper, did you ever find out who this Chrissy is?"

"No! No one on campus knows her."

"This is the second time her name came up in an investigation."

"Should I be alarmed?"

"Not at this time. I don't want to push the panic button unless there is a reason to.

And we are still looking into Paul Montgomery and Tiffany Powers. When we have more, I will let you know."

"Okay, thank you. Can I go now?"

"Yes. Don't go far. I may have more questions."

"OKAY."

"So, where do you think we should start?" asks Detective Berks.

"Well, I think we need to get all the reports back. Then ask the kids some questions. The first 2 we should start with are Paul Montgomery and Tiffany Powers. And try to find this Chrissy."

The evil one was quite pleased with how the liar succeeded in taking out the therapist. How it all went according to plan. "Now, as long as no one gets in my way, no one else will get hurt." The evil one says to himself.

All the kids were wondering what was going on. Juniper and the staff gathered all the kids together to try and calm everyone down.

"Settle down. I have something important to tell you.

The therapist Janet has been murdered. Before any questions are asked, we don't know what happened or if the 2 murders are connected. For now, until both murders are solved, no one can do anything alone. If you sit on the porch, someone must be with you. And if you see any-one on the property you don't know, tell staff immediately. Now, until the police finish up, everyone is confined to this area in case the police have questions."

Before Doc Matthews got in his van to head back to the morgue, Detective Deets had some questions to ask.

"Hey Doc Matthews, can you tell me anything at this time?'

"Well the only thing I am certain of is that acid was used. I don't know how or what kind. I hope to know more when I open up what is left of the victim."

"Okay, let me know as soon as you know anything!"

"I promise."

"Well, what do you think, Berks?"

"I don't know what to think. We have all her clients from here and 2 suspects from the last case, plus a new suspect that no one knows."

"I think we need to pray that forensics finds something to help us. This is no ordinary murder. Someone wanted this woman to suffer."

As forensics went over the murder scene, the crowd out-side waited patiently to hear some kind of news. Their sense of peace and safety was gone, now that 2 murders

happened in a short amount of time. Fear has begun to settle in.

Juniper was in her office shaking. She poured herself a
shot of vodka. She was shaking so bad her drink spilled
all over her clothes, leaving just a drop in her shot glass.
The Detectives started to ask the kids questions. Detective
Deets started with Paul as Detective Berks spoke to Tiffany.

"Okay, have you had any contact with the therapist,
Janet?

"No. I am new here. I really didn't really know that Jenn
girl who was killed well."

"Where were you Monday night?'

"Playing cards with my roommate Pete. He's over there
and will tell ya the same thing."

"Okay, that's all for now. I'm going to talk to your roommate, Pete."

"Pete? My name is Detective Deets, can I ask you a few
questions?"

"Yeah."

"Where were you Monday night?"

"My roommate Paul and I were playing cards."

"Did Paul leave at any time?"

"Nope!"

"Not even for a bathroom break?"

"Our bathroom is in our rooms."

"Did you know the therapist Janet?"

"I had 3 sessions with her."

"When did you last see her?"

"Monday at 10:00 A.M."

"Did she seem upset, nervous, or worried about anything?'

"She seemed fine to me."

"Okay, that's all for now. Do you know where I can find Mr. Nightwolf?"

"He is over there in a green shirt."

"Thank you!"

"Mr. Nightwolf, Detective Deets. Mind answering a few questions?"

"Why not."

"Where were you Monday night?"

"I had an appointment with the therapist Janet at 1:00, then went back to my room."

"So, you were the last one to see her?"

"No, there was a girl after me, who I didn't know."

"Can you describe her for me?"

"She has short black hair, no teeth, on the heavy side, a little taller than me, and had a 666 tattooed on her hands."

"Are you sure you've never seen this girl before?"

"I'm positive."

"If you think of anything else, even if it's small, don't hesitate to call me."

"Okay, I will."

"Detective Deets, did you learn anything new?" asked Detective Berks.

"Well, Paul Montgomery has an alibi. He was with his roommate Pete all night. Jose Nightwolf saw our victim at 1:00 P.M. She had an appointment after his about 2:00 p.m. He gave me a description of the girl who was after him whom he never saw before. I didn't ask him to look at photos. What about you, Detective Berks?"

"Well, Miss Powers was cocky and has no alibi. She claims she never was seen by the therapist because she doesn't need therapy. This is going to be another tough one. Let's hope Doc Matthews and Joe find something."

All at Pansy House were terrified. Two murders less than a month apart. Who would kill a therapist and a girl who bothered no one? Why is this happening? Who is next?

Ran through their minds. No one wanted to stay. Even Juniper and the staff wanted to leave. But they needed to be strong for the kids. A task they couldn't even do for themselves.

FRIDAY, AUGUST 17, 1990

At the station, Doc Matthews stopped in to fill the Detectives in on his findings.

"Detective Berks, I'm ready to give my findings."

"Alright, what can you tell us?"

"I found a small trace of tea in her stomach with an acid called Fluoroantiminic. This acid is very strong and fast acting. It eats up flesh like a fire in a forest. Now, what is surprising to me is that her organs remained intact. So, what I am thinking is when she drank the tea, she must have spilled it on herself, causing the acid to eat up her flesh. There wasn't enough in her stomach to eat her organs. If there had been, we would only have her teeth left."

"Do you have any idea where to buy this stuff?'

"The only place to buy it is online and you will have to do some research just to

find it."

"Wow! Thank you, Doc Matthews."

"Detective Deets, why don't we get to work on finding out who purchased this acid that is connected to Pansy House?"

"Sounds good to me. Hopefully we find something."

They spent the whole day researching this acid. At the end of the day, they came up empty. They were not ready to give up. Tomorrow is another day.

At Pansy House, life seemed to be at a standstill. No one left their rooms. Some were even terrified to even sleep. Except for Tiffany, she slept like a baby.

She got up, showered, went for breakfast, and sat on the porch for a smoke break.

She went about her business as if nothing happened. The staff members made sure the doors were locked and that everyone had their keys. Then they sat in their office waiting for Juniper to come in. They wanted to talk to her about closing down Pansy House with one, possibly more, killers on the loose.

"Good morning everyone! Is everything okay? I didn't expect the whole crew to be here."

"Well...." says Terry, a staff member, "We want you to consider closing Pansy

House until these murders are solved."

"You all feel that way?"

"Yes. "They all said at once.

"Well, I need to call my boss and see what he thinks, I can't make any promises.

I understand how you all feel. I am scared, too. I will do my best."

"That's all we ask."

"Tammy, can you give me this morning's report?"

"Sure! They all came down for breakfast and meds in pairs, except Tiffany. She acted like nothing happened and did not have a partner."

"Thank you! I will handle Miss Powers. I'd like us to check in on each room at least 2 times a day. Thank you all for not quitting on me and for coming in."

Juniper called her boss about closing Pansy House until the killer or killers are caught. She explained how the kids and staff were terrified to be there. How everyone was on lock down. How the killer is someone that no one has ever seen and the gruesomeness of each murder. Her boss agreed to closing down Pansy House.

Juniper gathered all the staff and kids together to tell them some good news.

"EVERYONE! PLEASE! QUIET DOWN SO YOU ALL CAN HEAR WHAT I HAVE TO SAY. I spoke to my boss and he has decided to close down

Pansy House just until the killer is caught."

They all began to talk at once. All couldn't wait to get home where they would be safe. Tiffany was not happy. Pansy House was closing. She had no place to go. But the evil one had a plan to get Paul to take her home.

"Hey, Tiff! Isn't it great that we get to go home?"

"I guess it would be if I had a home to go to."

"What do you mean?"

"Paul, I'm homeless, I will be right back to sleeping on a bench."

"Sorry to hear that."

"Hey Paul, do you think your dad will let me stay with you guys? I can pay rent and use my food stamps."

"I don't know, I will ask when I call."

"Okay, thank you, sweet pea."

"I hate that name."

The staff went back to their offices and packed up their personal stuff. And the kids went to call their parents before packing their stuff. Paul was on the phone with his dad begging him to allow Tiff to live with them.

"Hey Dad, you gotta come get me. They are closing down Pansy House."

"Paul, you are not coming home and that's final."

"But Dad, they really are! Here, talk to Juniper, she will tell ya."

"Hello, Mr. Montgomery, this is Juniper. Paul is telling the truth. Due to there being 2 murders and a killer on the loose, we have no choice but to close. Please come today."

"Now do you believe me?"

"Get your stuff together, I will be there in a bit."

"I was wondering if my girlfriend, Tiffany, can come live with us."

"I don't know! Doesn't she have family or friends she can live with?"

"Her family wants nothing to do with her and her friends are all men. Please.....? I promise she won't cause trouble and she said she will pay to stay with us and use her food stamps for food. I won't ask you for anything ever again!"

"Alright! Any problems and she goes. Let me talk to Debbie, I'm on my way. Hey,

Deb! Pansy House is closing so I need to pick up Paul and his girlfriend, Tiffany."

"Why Tiffany? Are you taking her to her parents?"

"No! Paul asked if she could stay with us. Apparently, she has no family who will take her in. And her friends are all men.nShe said she will pay rent and help with food."

"Hon, if her family wants nothing to do with her shouldn't that be a warning sign to us?"

"Look,I see what you mean. But we can really use the money and the food."

"I guess you're right. But if she turns out to be trouble, she goes."

"I already told Paul that."

Tiffany and Paul go to their rooms to pack everything up. The evil one was excited to see what trouble he could cause in a town where no one knows Tiffany. The evil one, manipulator, and the liar would get started as soon as they get to Pottstown.

As they were waiting for the parents to pick them up, they exchanged phone numbers with each other. Juniper let Detective Deets know that Pansy House was closing and where to find everyone. Juniper made it clear to everyone that these murders are open investigations. That she had to give the police their numbers and addresses, and if they move or change numbers to notify Detective Deets.

Bob, Paul, and Tiffany had a nice ride back to Pottstown. Bob kept asking Tiffany questions about her and her family. And Paul filled Tiffany in on who's who in the family.

"So, Tiffany, tell me about yourself."

"What would you like to know?"

"Well, about your parents, why you were at Pansy House, what do you like to do?"

"I've been on my own since I was 16. And I was put in Pansy House because I have bipolar disorder, anxiety, and depression. I like to live life to the fullest and to have fun."

"Okay... um....do you drink or take drugs?"

"Oh no, sir! I'm a good girl. I will help clean and cook. Whatever you need me to

do, I will do."

"Have you met the rest of the family yet?"

"No, I haven't. But I would like to."

"Maybe we can have a family get together, I will ask Paul's aunt. Her house is bigger than mine."

"Okay ,that sounds nice."

"Hey Tiff!" Paul chimes in. "I can't wait for you to meet my Aunt Joan. She tells it like it is. She tells people what she thinks. She is not afraid to open her mouth."

"What about me meeting your mom, stepdad, brother, and sister?"

"Then there's Grams, she also tells people what she thinks. If she doesn't like you, you will be the first to know. She has a funny laugh; her name is Isabelle. My brother Frankie is funny. He can make anyone laugh. He also is good at drawing. My sister Lynn, she is bad, she always gets her own way. My cousin Marie is the girl I stalked.

She is married to some guy named Brandon, he is a pastor of, "The one way to Heaven church."

Marie has a beautiful voice and can dance. My stepdad is an asshole. He does nothing but control my mom and bosses me around. My mom does nothing but play on her phone all day. Except she does whatever Sam tells her to do."

"Paul, don't talk about your mother like that! She does the best she can."

"Come on, Dad! You know I'm right."

"You only have one mother, remember that. Let's change the subject."

They were quiet the rest of the way home. Tiffany enjoyed the beautiful scenery. Green trees on top of small fields and amongst businesses and houses. The gorgeous blue sky. She couldn't wait to start over in a town where no one knew her and couldn't wait to start with this new family. Her goal is to ruin their lives.

They arrived at the Montgomery house just in time for dinner. They had Paul's favorite, spaghetti, salad, dinner rolls ,iced tea, and ice cream for dessert. Deb did most of the talking, asking questions and setting down the rules.

"So, Tiffany, tell me a little about yourself."

"Well, I've been on my own since I was 16. I have bipolar disorder. But I am on my meds. I like to have fun. I don't do drugs or drink. I do smoke. I like to help with housework. What else would you like to know?"

"I want to know how come your family won't take you in?"

"My parents abused me. My father raped me, and my mom did nothing to protect me, she allowed it to happen. When I reported it, my whole family was against me. My sister said I dressed sexy to provoke my father. I was put in foster care for a while, then I ran away."

"I'm sorry you had to go through all that. Let's get to house rules.

1. No smoking in the house. You and Paul are responsible to pick up the cigarette butts from the ground.
2. You both are expected to help keep this house clean.

3.You need to stay clothed at all times.
4.Don't be up all night. Some of us have to be up early for work.

"I understand and will respect your rules. How much would you like me to pay for staying here?"

"Well, you both need to pay $150 each month. That is what my daughter and

sister pay."

"Okay, no problem. Thanks for letting me stay."

"Just follow the rules and we all will get along."

Deb gave Tiffany a tour of the house. The attic, where Bob and Deb sleep, is a medium sized room with 2 small windows,a dingy whitish blue paint on the walls, and a full size bed which barely fits the 2. Above the bed was a hole in the ceiling with a fan-built in. They had 2 small dressers and a 13 inch TV in front of the bed. The kitchen was a huge eat in kitchen, with dull green paint on the walls.

There was a window that overlooked the driveway. There was a little island that came off the counter. Off to the right of the kitchen was a small bedroom with purple walls, a full-size bed and 2 big dressers. That is where Bob's dad, Joe, slept. The living room was a cozy little room with dingy yellow walls, and it had a musty odor to it.The bathroom, which was next to the living room, is small and quaint looking. There was a closed in porch which looked like it was never used. The room as you come into the house is a huge room, with the old-style paneled walls. This would be Tiffany and Paul's room, which they would be sharing with Deb's sister, Lori. There is a big car garage off to the side of the house, which is filled with trash and junk.

"My daughter, Kerri, and granddaughter, Kierena,sleep in

the living room. And you both have to share with my sister, Lori. Any questions?"

"I just want you to know how much I appreciate you allowing me to stay here."

"Don't think anything of it. Just follow the rules,and everything will be fine."

Deb and Bob went back upstairs. The evil one's wheels were turning on how to take over and destroy this family. All went to bed early; it was a long day.

SATURDAY,AUGUST 18,1990

At the station, Joe from forensics stopped by to give his report to the detectives. He had a confused look on his face. He didn't know if what he had would be good news or keep them at a standstill.

"Hey, Joe! Any good news for us today?"

"Well, Detective Berks, I don't know, that's up to you to decide. All fingerprints came back as staff or residents, but 1,a print we got off the glass of tea. When I ran it, it came up clean. But what was weird about this fingerprint is what was a part of the print. It was the number 666. So, I double checked the other crime scene fingerprints and found the same thing on a print from the ceiling fan."

"That means both murders are connected. So, we are looking for one killer.

Thanks Joe, you have been helpful."

"I wish we could have found more for you."

"Don't worry about it; you all did the best you could with what you had. Detective Deets, how about you search on murders with that fingerprint and I will continue the search on the acid."

"Sounds good to me."

Both detectives worked hard to come up with something. They ate lunch at their desks. It was just about quitting time when something came up.

"I GOT SOMETHING!" yelled Detective Deets."

"What is it?"

"There was a murder in 1940. In San Diego, California. The Jetson family of 5 were all murdered using the same acid the therapist Janet was killed with. But the only thing left was their teeth.

They had no suspects, and the only thing left at the scene was a 666 fingerprint. That was 50 years ago. The detective on the case died in 1994 of heart failure. And the case was considered dead, and they placed the case in Cold Case files. I wonder if we can gain access to those records."

"It's worth a try."

"Well... there is a website that sells unusual chemicals. I checked all the records and found that the acid was purchased by Chrissy Thompson. Her address is a post office box, which she closed 2 days ago. She paid cash."

"Great! Another dead end."

"Morning, Bob!"

"Hey hon, I'm going to give Joan a call to see about having a big family dinner at her place to introduce Tiffany to everyone."

"Are you sure about this? Something doesn't feel right about this girl."

"You just need to get to know her. It will be fine, you will see. Don't worry."

"I hope you are right."

"I'm going to call Joan."

"Hello!"

"Hey, Joan, how are you?"

"I'm good. Getting ready to take my mom shopping. What's up?"

"Paul and his girlfriend, Tiffany, are back here now. Pansy House closed due to some murders that took place there."

"That's terrible! Are they alright?"

"They are fine. I would like to get all of us together for a big family get together. Since your place is bigger than mine is, can

we have it at your place?"

"Do you mind if I invite Dan and Celeste and their family?"

"No, that's fine."

"Sounds good. Marie and I can make lasagna and spaghetti for the kids. How about Saturday? That will give me a week to get ready?"

"Okay, that will work. We will bring desert. Will 4:00 P.M. be good?"

"Yes, I will fill the rest in."

"Okay. Thanks Joan."

"Sam! Get everyone down here. I have something to tell everyone."

"What is it, Joan?"

"You will find out when everyone else does."

"Hey Mom, what's up?"

"I just got a call from Bob. He told me that Pansy House closed due to some murders that took place. And that Paul and his girlfriend Tiffany is living with him. We are having a big family dinner here, Saturday to meet this girl."

"Did he say what happened?"

"Damn it, Sam! I just told you what Bob told me. Listen when others speak and not just when you speak."

"Okay! Damn! I will give Bob a call and find out more."

"If there was more, don't you think he would have told me? I expect this place to be cleaned."

"I have a question to ask him anyway."

"Whatever! Nosey jackass! Come on, Marie, let's take Grams shopping."

"Can I come with, Aunt Joan?" asks Joan's niece, Lynn.

"Yeah, come on."

"I'm going to give Bob a call and see what I can find out." says Sam.

"Hey Bob, it's Sam. I hear you got him back and one more."

Sam laughs a goofy laugh.

"Didn't take long for you to call for information."

"Ha, ha, ha! So, I hear Pansy House closed. What happened?"

"I told Joan everything I know. They closed because of some murders."

"Oh, I know. Did they give you any information?"

"Nope!"

"How do you like the girl Paul brought home?"

"She seems nice."

"Did she tell you anything about herself?"

"She's been on her own since she was 16. Her dad raped her, and her mom did nothing to protect her. She was put in a foster home where she ran away. She has bipolar disorder. What else do you want to know?"

"Can I talk to Paul?"

"He took Tiffany to show her around Stowe."

"Can you have him call me?"

"As soon as I see him. Well, hey, I gotta go. See you Saturday."

"Okay, thanks, Bob."

"Who was that?" asked Deb.

"Just take a guess."

"Do I at least get a hint?"

"He has to know everyone's business."

"It must've been Sam."

"Yep! He wanted more information about Pansy House closing. I told him what I knew. So now he wants to talk to Paul."

"Did you get a hold of Joan?"

"Yes. They are making lasagna and spaghetti for the kids. I told her we would bring dessert. It's going to be this Saturday, 4:00 p.m. at her place."

Joan, Lynn, and Marie took Grams to the local mall shopping, then to the King of Prussia Mall. At the mall they stopped for lunch at the food court. Grams wanted to know more about Paul.

"Alright Joan, give me the scoop."

"What are you talking about, Mom?"

"I know Bob told you more than you told us."

"I told you everything!"

"Fine! Be that way. I'm not going Saturday."

"I'm staying in my room. You can't make me come down."

"Suit yourself. Joe will be there. And you'll miss finding out about this girl."

"Oh! Alright! I will come. But I'm not eating."

"Good! More lasagna for the rest of us."

"I'm not talking to you the rest of the day."

"So, mom, what is the menu?"

"Well, Marie, I figured you and I could make lasagna, salad, dinner rolls, the kids will get spaghetti. Can you tell Brandon no work on Saturday?"

"Mom, you know Brandon won't leave me when Paul is around after everything he put me through."

"I KNOW, BUT A PASTOR'S WORK DOES NOT STOP ON SUNDAY. IT'S

every day. Just make sure he is there. Mom, please be nice to this girl."

"Who the hell are you to tell me to be nice? I am 50 years old. I will do what I want!"

"Mom, please?"

"Whatever!"

"Well, let's get going to beat this traffic."

The ride home was quiet. When they got home, everyone went to bed. It was a long day. Tomorrow was church.

SUNDAY, AUGUST 19, 1990

At the police station in Bryn Mawr Detective Deets, follows up on a possible lead.

"San Diego homicide unit, Detective Child's speaking."

"My name is Detective Deets from Bryn Mawr PA, Homicide. I'm working on a case that is similar to a 1940 murder case of yours that is currently a cold case."

"What can I help you with?"

"I would like to know if you can send me whatever you have on the case?"

"What case is it?"

"Jetson, family of 5. Only thing left was their teeth."

"Let me transfer you to Cold Case."

"Thank you!"

"Cold Case, Detective Ford speaking."

"I'm Detective Deets from Bryn Mawr, PA, Homicide. I'm interested in a case from

1940."

"Can you give me more information?"

"It was a family of 5, the Jetsons. Only thing left was their teeth. The murder weapon was an acid."

"I got it! The only thing we have are the teeth and a 666 fingerprint found at the scene. There was one suspect, Chrissy Thompson. They didn't have enough to make an arrest."

"Did they question this girl?"

"No. It's like she vanished in thin air. The case is a dead end. I'm sorry, I wish there was more."

"Okay, you gave me more than you realize."

"Well, that was interesting."

"What did they say?"

"They pretty much have what we have. A 666 fingerprint, the same acid, and Chrissy Thompson as a suspect."

"How is that possible? That would make her an old woman now."

"I know, but that's all they had. We are at the beginning."

"Well I came up empty, too. The person always wore gloves when checking the

P.O. Box."

"What about the website?"

"That was a dead end."

"Well Detective Berks, it looks like we are at a standstill with both cases."

"Something will come up. This person will eventually make a mistake. They always do."

The Wert Family is a Christian family who has their own church. They go every Sunday, and that is where they are today.

The Montgomery family decided to stay home and just get to know this Tiffany girl better. Deb still has her doubts.

MONDAY, AUGUST 20,1990

It's Monday, there is a lot of work to be done for Saturday. With all the church activities, they needed to get an early start on the housework. Since Joan has OCD, that makes the cleaning more intense. The time is 8:00 A.M., Joan wakes up the whole house.

Everyone started complaining while Grams sat there and laughed.

"I want everyone to eat breakfast and gather in the living room when done." "Aunt Joan, it's summer. Why do we have to get up and clean?" yawned Frankie, Joan's nephew.

"Eat breakfast, then come into the living room and I will explain further."

It took 2 hours for everyone to eat and all met in the living room, where Joan told everyone what their jobs will be.

"On Saturday, we are having a lot of people over for dinner. This dinner is so we can all get to meet Paul's girlfriend. Any questions?"

"Does Marie really need to be here for this?" Brandon asks.

"I think she should be, yes. I know what Paul put her through. But things have changed, he has someone now. Anyone else?"

"He isn't moving in, is he Aunt Joan?" inquired Frankie.

"I told you a few days ago they are living at Bob's. I will be making lasagna and spaghetti for the kids. They are bringing dessert. Now, for housework. Marie and Brandon can clean the kitchen. Mom and I will take the living room. Sam, the laundry room. Kym, upstairs bathroom. Scott, the downstairs bathroom. Frankie and Lynn, the hallway and stairs and the back

yard. We all need to keep up with our rooms."

"Why do I always get stuck with Lynn?"

"Because I said so."

"Why can't they have us over there? I hate cleaning."

"Paul, Tiffany! Time to get up!"

"Dad, let us sleep some more. We were up late."

"That's not my fault. It's after 11 A.M. Deb has some things she wants done."

"Okay! We are getting up!"

"See you both later."

"Tiffany, we got some stuff to do.Get up!"

"I'm up! What needs to be done?"

"The kitchen and the living room. Which do you want?"

"Why don't we skip the cleaning and have sex all day?"

"What if someone comes in?"

"Then we cover up. PLEASE? Remember my promise to show you a good time?

Now is our chance."

"How about after we clean?"

"No! It's not our mess to clean up!"

"Fine....but, if we get in trouble, it's your fault."

"We can just say we didn't know she wanted us to clean. How will she know if we are lying?"

"True! This is my first time, what if I can't?"

"Don't worry, I can get any man to perform."

They stayed in bed the rest of the day. Deb was angry when she found them together. And even madder that nothing was done.

"WHAT IS GOING ON HERE? PUT SOME CLOTHES ON.BE THANKFUL MY GRANDDAUGHTER ISN'T COMING IN. YOU BOTH NEED TO USE YOUR DAMN HEADS WHEN

YOU DECIDE TO HAVE SEX. PEOPLE WILL ALWAYS BE IN AND OUT. AND

ANOTHER THING! YOU PROMISED ME TIFFANY THAT YOU HAD NO PROBLEM

HELPING AROUND THE HOUSE."

"Yes, I did, and I meant it."

"Then how come you didn't clean the kitchen or living room?"

"You didn't ask me to clean them or I would have."

"I told Bob what I wanted done and I came home to find you both in bed all day."

"I'm sorry, Deb. Bob nor Paul said nothing to me that work needed to be done."

"Are you telling me the truth?'

"I would never lie to you."

"Alright, I believe you. Next time you will be asked to leave. Understand?"

"Yes, I promise to do my share around here."

"Okay, now get some clothes on, the both of you, and come help me upstairs."

As they were getting dressed, the evil one says to himself, "This will be easier than I thought!"

"Hi honey! How was your day?"

"I had a good day until I came home and found Tiffany and Paul having sex.

Then I came upstairs and found that no house work was done."

"Do you want me to handle it?"

"I already did. Tiffany said you nor Paul told her I wanted her to do the kitchen or living room."

"When I woke up Paul, I told him you wanted the living room and kitchen done. He said okay."

"I told you I didn't feel right about bringing her here."

"Do you need to start this now!"

"I didn't mean to start. Let's just drop it. They should be coming up soon to help out."

"Tiff, why did you tell Deb that I didn't tell you we had to clean when I did?"

"Because, if I told her I chose not to clean I would get kicked out."

"Oh, I get it!"

"Let's go help before she starts her shit again."

Everyone worked hard to clean the place, even the kids. Sam was so curious about why Paul was really back, that he called Bob's to get information from Paul.

"Hello!"

"Who is this?"

"I'm Tiffany, who are you?"

"I'm Sam, Paul's step-dad. Is he there? I need to ask him something."

"Yes, he is .I will get him for ya."

"Paul! Sam is on the phone for you."

"What does he want?'

"He said he has to ask you something."

"Hey Sam, what do you want?"

"Why did Pansy House close?"

"You called about that? They closed because some people were killed."

"Did they say how and what happened?"

"I can't give out any more info because it's an open investigation."

"Okay. So, I hear you brought your girlfriend with."

"Yeah, she has no place to go. You will get to meet her Saturday. I gotta go."

"Tell your dad to call me."

"Whatever!"

"Did you find anything out, Sam?"

"No, Isabell, Paul said he couldn't give any information out because it is an open investigation."

"What does that mean?"

"It means the police have nothing to go on and the police don't want the public to know they are at a dead end."

"Oh! I'm hungry! What snacks do you have?"

"Joan will kill me if I give you ice cream at this hour."

"So, she has no say over me."

"Good night, Isabell."

(sticking her tongue out) "You wait till I get my check! I'll buy my own damn ice cream and you won't get any."

"I will give you some tomorrow."

"Oh, alright!"

All were asleep at both houses. It was a hot summer night. Bob's house had no air conditioning and the windows were painted shut. The only air was from individualized fans. Each person had only one, which blew the hot air that already was in the house. Tiffany had trouble sleeping, she was sticking to the sheets on the bed. She decided to sit up and watch Tv until 3A.M. From the noise of the Tv and Tiffany's laughing, Deb couldn't sleep. She went down to say something to Tiffany.

"Tiffany! Why are you up so late, making all this noise?"

"I'm sorry, I didn't know I was being loud. It's so hot, I'm having trouble sleeping."

"Can you please keep it down?"

"Okay, I will."

Deb goes back to bed. An hour goes by, (4:30A.M.), she wakes up to Tiffany's loud laughter. Not only did it wake her up, but the whole house. Kerri, Deb's daughter, went down to give Tiffany a piece of her mind.

"Look, bitch! Who the fuck do you think you are waking the damn house up? Don't you fucking realize people have to get up early?"

"Who are you calling a bitch? You have no clue who you are messing with. I will beat your ass."

"You think you're big and bad, let's go outside and see."

"You're not worth it! And I didn't wake everyone up on purpose. It's so hot that I couldn't sleep. Sorry I woke everyone. I'm a loud person. I will try harder to lower my voice."

TUESDAY, AUGUST 21, 1990

"I'm not worth it! I will take you out any day of the week. Try me. Next time, it's you and me."

"I ain't afraid of you, bring it!"

"ENOUGH! The both of you!" yelled Deb.

"This is your second day here, and you're making ene-mies already! I understand you can't sleep because of the heat. There is nothing anyone can do about the heat. The only thing I can suggest is for you to get another fan."

"I don't get paid for another 2 weeks! Can you buy one for me and I will pay you back?"

"Um.... I think I can, but I need the money back."

"Not a problem! Thank you!"

Since it was already morning, they decided to stay up and get ready for the day. Deb was off, so she decided to visit Joan and see if she needed any help getting ready for Saturday. It is Tuesday, 4 days to go. She asked Tiffany to clean the kitchen and Paul to clean the big room downstairs. Keri left to take Kerreana to day care, then off to work. Bob already left for work. As soon as Deb left, Tiffany went to bed. Since she was up all night, she needed sleep.

"Hi Deb! Is everything alright?" Joan asks as she opens the door.

"Well, I don't know. Can we talk?"

"Sure! Would you like some coffee, maybe a bagel or donuts?"

"Okay, thank you."

"What is on your mind?"

"You know that girl Tiffany, Paul brought with him?"

"Yeah, what about her?"

"She is causing problems already."

"Already? She just got here! What has she been doing?"

"Yesterday I asked Bob to tell Paul and Tiffany I wanted them to clean the kitchen and living room. I got home to them having sex. When I told her about it, she acted like it was no big deal and claimed she knew nothing about me wanting them to clean. What if Kerreana walked in? Last night, it was so hot, we all stuck to our beds. Tiffany had the tv up loud. It woke me up. I made her turn it down. Then about an hour later we all were woken up by her loud laughter. Kerri and Tiffany got at it. Tiffany seemed genuine when she apologized. I just don't have a good feeling about this."

"Have you spoken to Bob about how you feel?"

"I haven't had a chance to, with us both working and then taking care of Joe.

Things have gotten chaotic at my house."

"Joe is getting worse?"

"Yes, he is. He lost a lot of weight. I'm sorry for putting my problems on you. I really came here to see if you needed any help getting ready for Saturday."

"Nope we have it all together. Marie and I will get the main dish put together on Friday. My nephew and Brandon can put the pool up for the kids. Don't worry about telling me your problems. You needed someone to talk to."

"Thank you. How is Marie and everyone doing?'

"Marie has been having some problems with her stomach. Brandon is at the doctors with her now. Brandon's church is growing and growing. Kym still sits and plays on her phone. Sam is still nosey, having to be right all the time. Scott has become a lazy slob. Frankie and Lynn are good, and my mom has her good and bad days."

"Let me know what happens to Marie. I have been working and taking care of

Joe. We also help care for Kerreana. She is getting big. She loves her pop."

"That's great! How has Bob's health been?"

"He's been doing good. It's been 6 months since his last attack."

"Well Joan, I need to get home and make sure they did what I asked them to do."

"Stop by again. It was nice to see you."

"Okay! Let's do lunch sometime."

"Sure, see you Saturday."

Marie is home from her appointment. Isabell is on the porch enjoying the nice weather with Sam and Kym. The kids are at friends. Everyone was concerned about Marie's health, but was more concerned why Deb stopped over.

"How did your appointment go,Marie?"

"It went good, Mom. We won't know anything for sure until the test results come back."

"What did Deb want?" asked Sam.

"She is having some trouble with that Tiffany girl Paul is dating."

"Like what?"

"Well if you must know... She asked her to clean and came home to find them having sex and she woke everyone up last night with loud laughter. Kerri already got in her face about it. But Deb stepped in. Hey mom, Kym, and Marie, do you want to go to the store with me?"

"What are you going to the store for, Mom?"

"Well, I need to get stuff for Saturday, and I thought we would get a pool for the kids and you know, shop? Can you men clean up a bit?"

"Okay! Kym, get me deodorant and soda."

"I'm not getting you soda."

"Alright ladies and Lynn let's go. We are eating dinner out!"

"That's not fair!" complained Sam.

"You guys have money. Go out to eat yourselves. Alright ladies, let's go." Deb arrives home, walks in the house, and is angry at what she finds.

"WHAT THE HELL ARE YOU DOING? WALKING AROUND THE HOUSE

NAKED? GO PUT SOME CLOTHES ON RIGHT NOW!"

"ALRIGHT! DAMN! I cleaned the kitchen for you and all you do is bitch and yell at me."

"You are walking around my house naked! Right in front of Joe. And you act as if it's no big deal. What is wrong with you?".

"Joe didn't mind at all. And no one else was here. Plus, I did what you asked."

"Thank you for cleaning the kitchen for me. We will discuss this more when Bob gets home."

"I'm sorry, Deb! Give me another chance?"

"It will be discussed when Bob gets home."

As Deb and Tiffany are talking, Bob walks in unnoticed and just stood there with his mouth open.

"Like what you see, Bob?" asks Tiffany with a huge smile.

"Don't just stand there, Bob, tell her about it!"

"Um....Well...."

"Bob! Stop being googly eyed and say something.She can't get away with walking around nude. What if Kerreana came home early?"

"She's right, Tiffany, what the hell were you thinking? Running around the house nude?"

"I like cleaning in the nude. That way if I get dirty, I can hop right in the shower. Besides, it didn't bother Joe."

"Why would it? The man hasn't seen a naked woman in years. Go, get clothes on and come back so we can talk.'

"Bob, she has to go! She is causing too much trouble."

"We need to give her some time to get used to how we do things and to settle
into a stable home life."

"YOU PROMISED ME THAT SHE GOES IF SHE STARTS PROBLEMS! AND SHE HAS! SHE HAS TO GO!"

"Deb, it's only been a few days. Give her some time to adjust. Besides, Joan is working hard to make a good meal for Saturday. Let's wait until after that."

"FINE! No matter what, she goes!"

"Yes, I promise! Tiffany, can you come here for a minute?"

"Look, I am very sorry for walking around naked. I'm used to being nude when I clean. I didn't think about Kerreana coming in."

"How did you clean at Pansy House?"

"I made someone else do my chores."

"We are giving you some time to get used to things around here."

"Okay, thank you. You won't regret it."

"I hope not," replies Deb.

As night approaches, both families got dinner done, put the kids to bed. Joan and Isabelle watched movies together. Sam bored Kym with his Nascar racing. She played on her phone. Marie and Brandon were too excited to sleep. They went to the movies.

At the Montgomery House, Bob and Joe sat up watching baseball Kerri put Kerreana to bed and left with her boyfriend.Paul and Tiffany went for a walk. And Deb sat up talking to her sister, Lori, about what's been going on with Tiffany.

"How is it going with Paul's girlfriend?" "Well, for her first week here she sure is making herself known."

"What do you mean?"

"Things were good on Monday. Tuesday they were asked to clean the kitchen and living room. When I got home, I found them having sex and that no work had been done. She claimed no one told her I wanted them to clean. I got mad then let it go. That night, Tiffany was up all night. Apparently since she slept all day, she wasn't tired and with no fan it was too hot to sleep. The problem was, she kept the tv up loud. No one got any sleep. Kerri got pissed off and started an argument. I told her I would try to help her buy a fan. So that was settled. Then today I came home to a naked Tiffany. She cleaned for me like I asked. She has no respect for others or rules."

"Sounds like you had a rough few days. What has Bob said about all this?'

"He says I need to give her a chance. That she needs to adjust

to how we do things. He asked me to give her until after Saturday. Joan is having all of us over for dinner to meet Tiffany."

"Well, I can see his point in waiting until after the dinner. Joan is putting a lot of money and hard work into this dinner."

"I know she is. I'm stressed out more and more with her here."

"How does Paul feel?"

"He is so head over heels for this girl. He is thinking with his other head."

"I'm back now. I will help you anyway I can."

"Thank you, sis. I'm going to bed. Before I forget, they are in the basement with you."

"I figured that!"

On their walk together, Tiffany's mind was all over the place. The evil one is ready for the next person to kill. Who does this bitch think she is? Trying to get rid of us? She has no clue who she is dealing with. I'm in charge here." Her thoughts were interrupted as they walked in and saw Lori watching TV.

"Hey, Paul! How are you?"

"I'm good. Are you back to stay now?"

"Yeah, it was only for a few days anyway. Looks like we will be roommates! How do you like it here so far, Tiffany?"

"It's okay. Where will you be sleeping?"

"I thought I would take it by the door. Sometimes my boyfriend stops by. I wouldn't want to wake you."

"We want the other end anyway. Why are you watching our TV?"

"This tv belongs to me! I suggest you change that attitude around here."

"And if I don't?"

"I heard about what you've been doing. You need to know that you do not run the show around here. I will not let my

sister or brother-in-law have a heart attack over you."

"We will see who runs the show, won't we?"

"Tiff! Please don't start anything. My stepmom will put you out!"

"I ain't afraid of her or her fat slob of a sister. I will fight them both."

"Who are you calling a fat slob? Whore!"

"Bitch! You know nothing about me. I will cut you in your sleep."

"Tiffany! Stop it! Are you trying to get kicked out?"

"I'm sorry, she needs to keep her mouth shut."

"Look, you both need to watch your mouths."

"Paul is right, Tiffany. Let's start over."

The evil one is getting antsy. He begins to pick his next kill."Which one should I get first? Why not both at the same time?" The others chimed in. "That would be obvious." Says the evil one. "One at a time is best!"

WEDNESDAY, AUGUST 22,1990

It is a nice summer Wednesday morning. The birds were chirping beautiful music. The sky is a gorgeous mixture of blues, with huge billowy clouds. Today is a busy day at the Wert home. Joan has a lot to do before her niece and family come over. Her niece Celeste is a housewife married to Dan who has his own construction company. They have one child, Dan Jr, or jr. Marie and Celeste are more like sisters than cousins.

Marie could not wait for them to come. She had to tell someone her good news.

"Hey, Mom,what time is Celeste coming over?"

"They should be on their way. Why?"

"Oh nothing. I just want a girlfriend to chat with. And, Brandon wants to ask Dan to help him fix that wall in our room, and to help put the pool up."

"Sounds good."

"Aunt Joan! We're here!" yells Celeste.

"Come in. Hey, Jr., Dan. Why don't you go out back with Lynn? I have a surprise for you kids. Brandon is waiting for Dan in his room. Marie has been looking forward to seeing you.She's in the laundry room."

"Where's everyone else?"

"Frankie is in his room on his game system. Sam and Kym are hibernating. And

Scott went for his booty call."

"Aunt Joan!"

"What!? It's true! He goes to his cousins to sleep with his wife when he is at work."

"Where is Grams?"

"She's in the living room."

"Hey Celeste, come sit on the porch with me," yells Marie.

"Sure, it is nice out."

"Grams and I will be out in a few. I need to get her ready."

"Take your time, Mom."

"I know something is up, Marie. What is it?"

"If I tell you, promise not to tell anyone. Not even my mom or Dan."

"You know I won't."

"I went to the doctor the other day about my stomach. Brandon and I are having a baby."

"CONGRATS!"

"SHHH! Mom will hear you."

"Sorry! Why don't you want anyone to know? That's great news!"

"We are announcing it Saturday at the dinner we are having."

"What dinner?"

"Paul came home from that place he was in and brought this girl with. His family and ours are having a dinner here to meet her."

"I wanna come! Oh, before I forget, looks like we will be raising our kids together."

"Ask Mom if you can come. You're pregnant, too?"

"Yes!"

"CONGRATS!"

"Congrats to what?" asks Joan.

"Aunt Joan, I was telling Marie that I'm having another baby."

"Good for you. Do you know how far you are?"

"Not until next week. So.... Aunt Joan, I hear you are having a big dinner on
Saturday."

"You did, huh? Well I was going to ask you today if you guys would like to come."

"You know I will be here. I love your cooking. Has any-one seen this girl yet?"

"Only this picture."

"OMG! She looks like Marie! He's taken this obsession with Marie to a whole new

level."

"We know. I'm hoping he stays with this girl long enough to get over Marie."

"I hope so, too, Aunt Joan. Hi, Grams!!"

"Where's my great grandson?"

"He is out back with Lynn. I hear you are having com-pany over on Saturday."

"Well, I'm not coming!"

"Yes, you are, Mom!"

"You're not my boss. I can do what I want!"

"Please, Grams? I'm coming and I have good news."

"Oh? What?'

"I'm pregnant!"

"Again! Fine! But I'm not being nice."

"Thanks, Grams!"

"Whatever! So, Marie, when is your baby due?"

"Ahhh....why...why would you ask me? I'm not pregnant. Celeste is."

"You are glowing. That means baby."

"It's this new lotion I bought."

"I'm not stupid. What did the doctor say?"

"Leave her alone, Mom. She already told us the doctor ran tests. Besides, she would be jumping for joy if she were pregnant."

"Okay,you wait and see. I know more than you think I do."

"Alrighty then! Let's change the subject."

"Need some help?"

"Hey, Dan! I was hoping you would help me. Joan has a pool for us to put up for the kids."

"What happened here?"

"The rain was coming in through the outside wall, soaked the inside wall, and it collapsed."

"Did you fix it from the outside first?"

"Yes."

"Let me see what I can do."

"Thanks, Dan."

"So, what's been going on?"

"Paul is home from that home he was in, and he brought a girl home with him."

"Good! Then he will leave Marie alone."

"Well, I don't know about that. This girl looks a lot like Marie."

"That's sick!"

"Joan is having a lasagna dinner on Saturday for everyone to meet her."

"I would love to see that. We weren't invited."

"You know Celeste already invited herself."

Laughing, Dan says, "True! So, anything else happening?"

"Well, I got some good news, just promise me you won't tell anyone."

"Can I tell Celeste?"

"I'm sure Marie already has. Those 2 are thick as thieves."

"That's true! What's up?"

"Marie and I found out the other day that we are having a baby."

"That's great news! That's funny, because Celeste just found out she is pregnant. Why don't you want anyone knowing?"

"Marie wants to tell everyone at the same time. Which will be at the dinner

Saturday."

"That makes sense, since we all will be at the same place."

"Ready to put the pool up?'

"Sure."

At the Montgomery house, things were calm for the moment. Everyone got up and decided to hang out. They wanted to get to know Tiffany. And Tiffany needed to know them so the evil one can work his magic.

"Lori, what are all those lotions for? Do you collect them?"

"I use them all. I love to smell nice. One day I will use this rose one, another day gardenia, and another straw-berry splash. I wear the strawberry splash more. That's my favorite."

The evil one's wheels are turning. "If only there was some kind of stuff to mix in

her lotions to kill this bich."

"That's good to know for when I buy you a gift. What do you do around here?"

"Well there's bowling, golf, a place to go swimming, a theater, and a mall."

"NO! I mean, what do you personally do?"

"I am on disability and I am taking my GED. I go to the local college."

"I'm on disability, too."

"Why are you with Paul?"

"Because we are in love."

"You haven't known him long enough to fall in love."

"I fell in love with him the first moment I met him."

"PLEASE! Don't give me that crap! You were dating and pregnant when you both met."

"Doesn't mean anything! I love him and he loves me and there's nothing you or anyone else can do about it! So yeah!"

"You misunderstood, I was just stating the facts."

(Hearing loud voices, Paul rushes downstairs)

"What's going on?"

"Lori called me a liar about us loving each other."

"What does she know about love? Her man is with her for a place to live. He is an ex-con."

"So yeah! Mind your own business."

"You know what whore! You are on borrowed time here. We will see who has the last laugh."

"Leave my girlfriend alone. This is me, my dad, and my pop pop's house. If anyone is leaving it's you."

"Yeah, so step off!"

"You know what Paul, this slut is only with you because you have somewhere to live. Wait and see, your life is ru-ined."

"Whatever, fat ass!"

(THIS BITCH IS MESSING WITH THE WRONG PERSON. SHE WILL BE THE

FIRST TO DIE. Thought the evil one.)

"How about this, you both leave me the fuck alone, and I will leave you alone?" "Fine with us, bitch!" replies Tiff.

"DINNER'S DONE!" yelled Deb.

"Alright! Be up in a minute, sis."

"Hey, sis! What's for dinner?"

"Hot roast beef sandwiches, mashed potatoes, and a salad"

"Sounds good."

"Let's eat!"says Bob

"Give me the damn roast beef, whore!" Lori says to Tiffany.

"Here, have some potatoes with it." Tiffany dumps the food on Lori's lap.

"What the hell are you doing, tramp?

"Tiffany! What the hell are you doing? That's dinner for the rest of us, too."

"Sorry, Deb. Your sister said some mean things to me. I was getting even."

"That was everything I made for dinner. What will we eat now?"

"Don't worry hon, I will order pizza."

"That's not the point! She needs to handle herself without destroying things and hurting the rest of us. She really needs to go! What did Lori say that was so mean you had to waste the food Bob and I pay for?"

"She told me that Paul and I couldn't love each other, we just met. That I'm using

Paul for a place to live."

"Are you using Paul?'

"NO! I love him very much."

"That's not a good reason to waste my food. So, since we just spent an extra

$40 on dinner that we didn't need to. You will give me an extra $40 in rent."

"That's not fair! What about Lori?"

"You're the one who dumped the food."

"Whatever! I'm not done with you, bitch!"

"I ain't afraid of you, little girl. Bring it!"

"ENOUGH! THE BOTH OF YOU!" Yelled Bob, "If you both keep this fighting up, the both of you will be kicked out! Now you both can clean the kitchen."

"Tell me when her half is done."

"I meant together, Lori.'

"FINE!"

Twenty minutes after they began to clean up, Lori breaks the silence.

"Tiffany, I'm sorry for the things I've said to you. Can we start over?"

With a devilish grin and a plan, Tiffany agrees to start over. Because as they were cleaning the kitchen, Tiffany found a bot-tle of boric acid. She read the label and it's used to kill bugs.

"This will work perfectly." The evil one says to the ma-nipulator. "All you need to do is get lotion in a brand she doesn't have, put some boric acid in the bottle. Pretend to be a lotion salesperson. When she puts on the lotion, no more Lori!"

The kitchen was cleaned, the pizza came. They ate din-ner and everyone went to bed. All Tiffany could think about was getting rid of Lori.

"Let's see..." Says the evil one. "How about the salesman drops by Friday about noon. Pay attention, manipulator. This has to be done right the first time."

"I know it does. You stress too much. Relax."

"Just do everything I say to the T."

"I will."

THURSDAY, AUGUST 23, 1990

Thursday, one more day after this then the big day is here .At the Wert household it's food pantry day.

"Good morning, Mom!" Says Brandon.

"Hey Brandon, I know today is food pantry day, but I need to get some stuff done for Saturday.""Did you forget we are closed today because of the FDA inspection of our kitchens?"

"Yeah, I did."

"It's okay, it's still early."

"What would you like me to do?"

"Well... make sure the folding tables and chairs are cleaned."

"Sure, so, did Celeste ask to come?'

"Yes! I was going to invite her anyway. Saturday should be interesting. I'm worried about how my mom will behave."

"Don't worry, it will be a good day. Let's take a moment and pray about it.

Father, God, we ask for your strength to get through Saturday. We put the whole day in your hands. May the conversations we have and the things we do reflect who you are to us. Please keep Mom calm as she does all the preparations. In Jesus' name we pray, Amen!"

"Thank you, Brandon. I needed that. It's all going to be okay."

Everyone else is up and ready to go. Hoping Joan goes easy on them today, knowing the next few days will be hell on them.

"Hey, Mom, what's up for today?"

"Well, I thought you, me, Grams, Lynn, and Kym would come with to get the rest of the supplies we need for Saturday."

"You're taking Kym?"

"Well... I don't feel like fighting with Sam."

"Fighting with Sam about what?"

"Not taking Kym shopping with us."

"She won't help with anything. She's useless."

"Now, Mom!"

"What? It's true!"

"Yeah, you're right! Let's just get it over and done with. Marie, can you get Lynn and Kym? Tell them I want to get going."

"Sure, Mom.""

"So, Brandon, tell the truth. Marie is pregnant, isn't she?"

"Grams, she's not pregnant. The doctor would have told us .Besides, we are still waiting for the test results."

"Test results, my ass! They can do them right in the office."

"If she was pregnant, we would be so excited and would've said something."

"What are we talking about?"

"You being pregnant.'

"Grams, I would've said something!"

"Okay! I will drop it for now."

"Okay, let's get going. Are they ready?"

"Yes, Mom. Where are we going?"

"Well, I think going to BJ's will be cheaper for the lasagna dinner. I'm making spaghetti and meatballs for the kids. Then maybe go to Walmart. And then out to lunch."

"Aunt Joan, can we go to Bob Evans?"

"We sure can."

They went to BJ's. Picked up lasagna and spaghetti noodles, sauce, meatballs, and kielbasa, garlic knots, salad, dressing, soda, juice, tomatoes, cucumbers, and croutons. Deb and Bob are picking up the dessert. Joan loves to go all out and

decided to get watermelon, cantaloupe, some other fruits, and a veggie tray. She also picked up food for the house. Now they are headed to Bob Evans for lunch.

"Welcome to Bob Evans, how many people in your party?"

"Um...5."

"Follow me. What would you like to drink?"

Marie-tea with lemon, Joan-Pepsi, Isabelle-tea, Kym-root beer and

Lynn-Pepsi."Your waiter will be with you shortly."

"So, Kym, did you meet this girl when you dropped Paul off?"asks Joan.

"Yeah, just to say hi.She seemed nice."

"I hope she's not using Paul. From the trouble she's been causing at Deb's house, I'm anxious to meet this girl."

"I'm just glad Paul found someone to date so he leaves me alone. Does anyone else find it creepy that this Tiffany looks like me?"

"Well, I do. But you are prettier than she is. Are you sure you are not pregnant? You are glowing."

"Grams, if I was pregnant I would be overjoyed and couldn't wait to tell everyone.

Can we drop it?"

"Okay, wait and see. When do you get the test results back?"

"When the doctor calls with them."

"Enough, Mom! Let's order our food. Waitress!"

"Are you ready to order?"

"Yes, we are. Joan-I will have the hot roast beef sandwich, a salad, and a biscuit. Marie-I will have the 5 cheese penne with chicken, broccoli, a salad, and a biscuit. Isabelle- I want the fried chicken breast, mac and cheese, a salad, and a biscuit. Kym-I will have the hot turkey sandwich with a salad and a biscuit. And Lynn- I want a cheeseburger with fries. I will take these.

Your food will be right out."

As the ladies were enjoying the food and each other's company, Sam calls Joan with a problem.

"What do you want, Sam? Can't Kym do anything without you?"

"Joan, this is serious. Fat Boy called and said if someone doesn't get Marc today, he is putting him out on the street."

"He is only 16! Why is he kicking him out?"

"Something about him walking around the house in his boxers, eating up the food, and he wouldn't follow the rules. I only know what Fat Boy is saying."

"Call him back and tell him I will be there in 45 minutes. We are almost done.

Send me the address."

"Come get me and I will show you where he lives."

"I'm not coming all the way back home then back this way for Marc."

"I thought you were in Bechtelsville? Where are you?"

"Eating lunch at Bob Evans in Oaks. I got everything here at BJ's."

"That's a bunch of bullshit!"

"You guys could've gone out!"

"Whatever! I will tell him you're on your way. I will send you his address."

"Thank you!"

"What did he want?" asks Isabelle.

"Fat Boy is kicking Marc out!"

"Isn't he only 16, Mom?"

"Yes, that is why I'm picking him up."

"Where will he sleep, Mom? We are already full."

"I can put him in the spare room off Frankie's room. Let's head out!"

The ride to Fat Boy's trailer in Trooper was quiet. Each wondering how anyone can put a 16 year old out on the street.

"Well, here we are. You guys can stay in the vehicle. I will deal with this mess."

"Mom, behave!"

"I will try. Hey Marc, where is your uncle?"

"I will get him. Fat Boy! Aunt Joan is here."

"Let's cut to the chase. What is going on?"

"Well Marc isn't listening. He walks around the house with just his boxers. He yells and hits JR. He cuts down Patrick's religion. I can't get him to do anything."

"Well, if I take him, you would have to sign his checks over to me and sign all rights over to me"

"Okay. Are you calling Ruth, or should I?"

"Nope! I will take care of everything. Let's talk to Marc. Marc, if you come live with me, you will be expected to go to church, do chores, and follow the rules. Do you under-stand?"

"Yes, Aunt Joan."

"I'm serious! I'm not playing the same game your uncle played."

"Okay! Geeze."

"And another thing, I don't do attitudes."

"Alright!"

"Okay, I gotta go. I have a lot to do for Saturday."

"What's Saturday?"

"Paul's home from that home and he brought a girl with. We are having a dinner to meet her."

"Where's my invite?"

"You wouldn't come anyway."

"True! That's good he found someone. Now he can leave Marie alone."

"Well, I don't think that will happen. This girl looks like Marie. Here is a picture."

"OMG! They look alike. He's taken this to a new level. And the cops won't help?"

"Not unless he makes threats or does bodily harm."

"That is not right. What if he kills her?"

"I know. Listen, I need to get going."

"Okay, sis, call and let me know how Marc is doing."

"I will."

The ride home was filled with questions to Marc. Asking, "What is the real reason he was being kicked out?" Joan didn't like what she heard. But there was nothing she could do. At the house, everyone helped unload the SUV. Of course, Sam needed to know everything. Joan filled him in with what she thought he needed to know. Everyone settled in for the night. Frankie told Marc the rules for his room, since he would have to walk through Frankie's room to leave his room. Joan got her mom showered and ready for bed. Sam called Fat Boy for information but learned nothing. The rest of the family watched movies together then off to bed. All knew the next 2 days would be crazy.

FRIDAY, AUGUST 24, 1990

Friday, tomorrow is the big day! Joan and Marie were getting the lasagna made so that all that they needed to do was pop it in the oven. Bob went to get drinks and dessert. The manipulator was already putting the plan into action. He bought 5 different lotions. Changed the labels then put boric acid in all of them and made sure they were completely mixed, waited till noon, then, showtime.

"May I help you?"

"I would like to speak to the one who wears lotion."

"That would be me."

"And what is your name, pretty lady?"

"Lori."

"Hi Lori, my name is Stan. I work for Beautiful Skin Lotions. Can I come in and show you our lotions?"

"Sure, let's see what you have."

"Let me ask you this, what is the fragrance of lotion you wear the most?"

"That would be strawberry splash."

"Great! Our brand is called strawberry parfait. Would you like to smell it?'

"Yes, please."

"Great! Compare the smell of what you currently have to ours."

"Yours has a powerful strawberry scent which is stronger than what I am using. I

like that."

"Would you like to buy some?"

"How much are they?"

"Today we are running a special, $2 a bottle."

"That's cheap! I'll take 5 bottles."

"Great, $10 please."

"I can't wait to try it."

"You will love it and so will your friends. You have a nice day."

"Thank you. You, too!"

"I can't wait to try this new lotion tomorrow."

"Hey Lori, who was that?" asked Deb.

"Some lotion salesperson. I bought this lotion with a powerful strawberry scent!" "Let me smell it. It does have a powerful strawberry scent.

Did you put some on yet?"

"I already have the gardenia one on. I'm putting some on for tomorrow."

"Okay. I'm going to clean the living room."

Lori got all her stuff ready for tomorrow's dinner. She was planning on wearing this peach capri outfit with sandals. Deb got her cleaning done then decided to get her outfit for tomorrow ready. A teal outfit with white flats. Bob went to bed early. Paul and Tiffany had trouble sleeping. Tiffany's thoughts were all over the place. First, she thought about what the house would be like without Lori. Then she worried about tomorrow's dinner. Would she be accepted or will they turn Paul against her? Paul was excited to show off his real life girlfriend. No more pretending, no more chasing a woman who doesn't want him. He was now a man.

At the Wert household, all the food was ready to go. The tables were set up with table settings. The pool was up and running, the yard was clean, everyone knew to bring their suits and towels.

Each person did their share of work. Marc was nervous about living with his aunt whom he heard stories about. Not all good. Brandon and Marie couldn't wait to share their good news with everyone. Joan and Isabelle went to bed early. Sam and Kym sat up talking. The kids were excited to meet this girl who looks like their cousin Marie.

SATURDAY, AUGUST 25,1990

The big day is finally here! Lori got up, took her shower, and started to put her new lotion on. She put it all over. Heavy on the dry skin.

"Hey Tiff, want to try some of my new lotion?"

"NO! Thanks for asking. It smells good though. What is it?"

"It's strawberry parfait."

"I will try it another time."

"Sure, you better get ready."

"I'm ready. Do you think they will like me?'

"If Joan or her mother, Isabelle, don't, you will know it. They have no trouble telling you. Be careful of Sam, he is nosey and a trouble maker. He also is nice to your face, then trash talks you behind your back. Kym is spineless. Marie and Brandon are upfront, too. Just be yourself, don't go to impress."

"Thanks, Lori."

Lori began to itch from the lotion and just put more on where she was itching. Everyone else was getting ready to go. Tiffany was getting nervous, not knowing what to expect. Will she be accepted with open arms, or will they treat her like she is the dirt beneath their feet? Either way she would be ready for them. One way or another no one will stop her plans on taking over this family. Paul walks in and interrupts her thoughts.

"Hey beautiful! Are you ready to go?"

"I'm worried about meeting your mom and stepdad."

"Don't worry my mom will love you. I don't give a damn what Sam thinks. The people I worry about is my Aunt Joan and Grams."

"Why don't you like your stepdad?"

"Because he treats me like I'm nothing and is always causing trouble. He bosses my mom around and spends her money. When you get to know him, you will see."

The Montgomery house is already to go. Time to load up the drinks and the desserts.

Things were going smoothly at the Wert house. Dan, Celeste, and JR showed up early to help with the food and other preparations. Spaghetti, meatballs, and kielbasa needed to be made for those who don't like lasagna. The salad had to be made yet and the drink fridge needs to be stocked.

Joan got her mom ready. Marie's excitement about telling everyone the good news kept growing with each coming hour. Sam and Kym put on nice clothes for them and got Lynn ready. Frankie did not feel he should not have to attend the dinner. Marc kept to himself, this was all new to him. 12:00 noon, time for the games to begin.

"Alright everyone, they should be here any moment. Mom, be nice."

"Who are you talking to? I'll say what I want!"

"Mom...please?"

"Fine! Just this once. Hey Marie, I got my fingers crossed, don't say anything."

"Grams!"

"Alright, here they all are. Hi, guys! Let's go into the living room."

They all gather in the living room for introductions.

"This is Tiffany. Tiffany, this is Paul's mom, Kym, step-dad, Sam, his brother, Frankie, and sister, Lynn. Over here is his Aunt Joan, Grams or Isabell, Marie, and her husband, Brandon .Joan's niece, Celeste, her husband, Dan, and son, Dan Jr. Their

friend, Scott. Oh, Marc's here."

"Yes, my brother kicked him out on Thursday. It's nice out, why don't we enjoy the porch. So, Tiffany, tell us about you."

"What would you like to know? Can I call you Aunt Joan?"

"Sure! Anything you feel we should know."

"Well, I have been on my own since I was 16 years old. Most of my friends are men. I was engaged to be married. But when I lost the baby, he left me. I was put in Pansy House because of being homeless and having bipolar manic depression. I love to sing, and I love Paul."

"Are you saved?"

"Saved?"

"Yes! Have you accepted Jesus as your personal Savior?"

"Um....I believe in God."

"There is a difference between believing in God and Jesus being your personal

Savior."

"You're right! I'm sorry, I'm very nervous."

"It's a simple question. You either are saved, or aren't you?"

"Mom?" Says Marie. "You made Grams promise to be nice, you be nice. Don't mind her, she's blunt and to the point."

"Well, are you?" Joan asks again.

"Yes, I am saved. It is really none of your business."

"No, it's not but I like to know who I am dealing with."

"What I want to know is why are you really with Paul? "Grams chimes in.

"Well, Grams...."

"It's Isabell to you."

"Isabell, I love Paul and hope to marry him someday."

"You don't love Paul. You're only with him because of his check and he has a

place to live."

"I am truly and deeply in love with Paul. I don't care what he has. And Paul loves me. Ain't that right, Paul?"

"Yes, Grams, we deeply love each other."

"You only love her because she is your first piece of ass."

"Look, if you can't handle that Paul chose me over Marie, then that's on you."

"Little girl, you have no clue what you're talking about. Shut your mouth before I punch it!"

"MOM! ENOUGH! Don't mind her, she hasn't taken her meds yet."

"It's okay, I understand. (Who does this old bitch think she is? She better watch her back. The evil one is already adding Grams to the kill list.)

"Don't apologize for me. I'm telling the truth! I'm not shutting up for anyone. Hey Lori, you smell nice, what kind of perfume are you wearing?"

"Oh, this is not perfume. It's a new lotion I bought, called strawberry parfait. I have it with me, would you like to put some on?"

"No, I already have some on. Where did you get it from? I want to buy some."

"A salesman came to the house."

"Did you get a business card?"

"No, and I didn't think to ask for one."

"It looks like your arm is bleeding, Lori." Grams says.

"Oh, damn it! Joan, do you have a band aid?"

"I need to get dinner ready anyway. Come and I will give you my first aid kit. Marie, Celeste, can you help me get the food ready? Dan, can you have the kids come in and wash their hands?

"Joan, can we help with anything?" asks Deb.

"We got it! Can you help my mom to her seat and keep her out of trouble?"

"Sure! Come on, Isabelle, let's seat you at the end."

"Aunt Joan, how do you want the food displayed?"

"Um....let's put it in the center then we can pass it around. Parents, I made spaghetti for the kids and for those who don't like lasagna. There's salad, broccoli with cheese, and garlic knots. Drinks are in the drink fridge in the laundry room. Brandon, when everyone is seated, say grace for us."

"Sure thing, Mom. Let's bow our heads to pray. Father, God, we thank you for this food you have blessed us with. Bless the hands that have prepared it for us, bless the family and friends who are joining us this fine day. May our conversation be pleasing to your ears. In Jesus' name we pray, Amen." Before we begin, Marie and I have some news we want to share. Go ahead,honey."

"You all know I've been having stomach trouble. I went to the doctor and he ran some tests. Brandon and I are having a baby."

"I knew it! I told you she was pregnant. No one ever listens to me."

"Yes, Grams, you were right."

Everyone said congratulations, but Tiffany was angry. This was to be her day, no one else's. Who does Marie think she is stealing her spotlight? I will get even. Tiffany was deep in thought as Celeste was talking to her.

"Hey Tiffany, do you have any children? Tiffany, are you listening?"

"Sorry, I was deep in thought. What was your question?"

"Do you have any children?"

"I have 3 children that my mom has custody of. I never get to see them."

"Sorry to hear that, what kinds of things do you like to do?"

"I like to hang out, go shopping, really anything that is fun."

"You should hang out with me and Marie. I'm going to have a baby shower for
her."

"That's nice of you. So, tell me about your family. Your husband and son."

"Well, my husband Dan has his own construction business, we have 1 son and a baby on the way. I am a stay at home mom. I have a sister and a brother. We are a close family."

"Okay, what about Marie?"

"Let me have her tell you herself. Hey, Marie, tell Tiffany some things about you and Brandon."

"Well, Brandon is the pastor of One Way to Heaven Church, which is located on Gay Avenue. I also work at the church. We have Sunday school and chapel services. We serve lunch once a week and a food pantry,. Stop in sometime. Brandon and I have been married for a year. This is our first child. We are saving money for our own place. How long do you plan on staying with Paul and Deb?"

"Well, I'm hoping Paul and I will have our own place someday."

"Have you started looking?"

"Well, not really. Paul doesn't know my plans yet."

"Have you thought about staying where you're at until you get money saved?"

"Well, I get along with his dad and pop pop, but his stepmom and aunt don't like me."

"Sorry to hear that! What's the problem?"

"Well his stepmom is constantly yelling at me, she doesn't appreciate how I try to help around the house. And her sister lays in bed naked all night with no covers, and we have to share the same room with her."

"Sorry to hear you are going through all that. Have you tried talking to Bob and

Deb about it?"

"Yeah, I have, Bob defends his wife, and Deb told me her sister was there first to deal with it or leave. I have no other place to go."

"That's not right! You are a guest in their home. They should treat you better. Let me say something to my mom. She and Deb are friends."

"Thank you! I appreciate it."

"So, Tiffany, do you have a job or any income?"

"Well.... What is your name again?"

"Joan."

"I get SSI for bipolar."

"Have you thought about working part-time?"

"I guess, I mean, I really haven't thought about it. I need to get to know the area some more before I go to work."

"I understand you wanting to get to know the area more. But shouldn't you and Paul start saving money for your own place? I mean Bob and Deb are putting you up for the time being."

"Look,you don't know me well enough to judge me. I appreciate them taking me in. I'm not using them."

"You got it all wrong. I'm not judging you. I'm saying you and Paul should start putting money away for your own place."

"I'm sorry! I'm stressed. I have only been here a week and Deb and her sister have gone out of their way to make my stay miserable. They've attacked me since I've gotten here. You're not who I am here to meet anyway. Sam and Kym and their kids are."

"LISTEN HERE, TRAMP! YOU ARE A GUEST IN MY DAUGHTER'S HOME,AND

YOU WILL TREAT HER WITH RESPECT! SHE DIDN'T HAVE TO HOLD THIS DINNER FOR YOU. YOU DON'T SEE ANYONE ELSE WANTING YOU HERE. KYM HASN'T SAID A WORD TO YOU. SHE'S BEEN ON HER PHONE. AND SAM ONLY CAME DOWN TO EAT.HE'LL STAY DOWN NOW THAT I SAID SOMETHING. NOW, SHOW SOME RESPECT OR GET THE HELL OUT!" yells Grams.

"AND WHO THE HELL DO YOU THINK YOU ARE TELLING PEOPLE THAT

WE TREAT YOU HORRIBLE? TRY TELLING THE DAMN TRUTH! I CAN NOW IF

YOU WANT," says Deb to Tiffany.

Turning on the water works, Tiffany says, "I'm sorry, you're right. I didn't mean to be rude. I've been dealing with a lot lately. Like I said, Deb and Lori made this week hell for me. All I tried to do was help. I am still trying to get over the loss of my baby and fiancé in the same day. The murders at Pansy House. Now a new family. It's a lot in a short time. Please forgive me, Aunt Joan? Can we start over?"

"We can start over. How have Lori and Deb made this week hell for you? I won't apologize for looking out for my family and friends. We know nothing about you. So you had to expect to be interrogated."

"I don't want to start anything here. Can I stop over this week and talk to you about it?"

"Well, you already started it, but you're right, there are children here. Paul has my number, give me a call or stop by."

Butting in, Sam says, "So, where are you from?"

"I'm from all over. I've lived in New Jersey with my aunt. Tennessee with other family. I was born in Bryn Mawr and grew up in Norristown."

"Where abouts in New Jersey?"

"Well mainly Camden. My uncle has his own snack food company."

"Which one?"

"Wackie O's. It's by the highway."

"I used to deliver food there when I drove truck for my dad. Have you ever been in that place? It's huge!"

"No! I was a small child. I just know that he owns it."

"Sam will bore you to death with his questions and trucking stories. Just tell him to mind his own business."

"Funny, Paul! So how long did you live in Camden? Do you know the area well?"

"I told you I was a small child. I haven't been back because my parents moved a lot. All you need to know is that I was at Pansy House, and now I am living in Pottstown."

"Have you ever been to the Camden Aquarium?"

"Sam, didn't you hear what Tiffany said?"

"Yes, Joan I did! I'm just trying to get to know her."

"Tiffany, just write down your whole life so Sam can know everything about you.

Lori, are you okay? Brandon, get my first aid kit.The one I use for Grams. Hurry!"

"I'm okay, Joan. Please don't make a fuss."

"It's no fuss at all. It will only take a minute. I will bandage your arm. You will need to see a doctor. What happened?"

"It's nothing, Joan, please don't take the time away from dinner. I've been scratching a lot today. I just need to get used to this new lotion."

"It's not a problem. It won't take away from dinner. Everyone is done anyway. Let me just wrap your arm up."

"Oh! Okay, thanks Joan."

"It's no problem."

Tiffany was trying hard not to laugh or smile. Soon no more Lori, she thought to herself. Throughout the day, more and more skin came off. She was able to keep it from the rest of the family. Celeste, Marie, Deb, and Tiffany cleared away the dishes and the food. The men got the kids ready to go swimming. Then they sat on the porch talking. Tiffany was talking to Brandon and Marie about their church.

"So, Brandon, tell me about your church."

"Hands off, gold digger! He's married!"

"Grams! Behave!"

"I'm reminding her, that's all."

"Don't mind Grams, she needs to get to know you better. What would you like to know?"

"Anything! I would like to come check it out sometime."

"Well we have a Christian church. Which means we believe that Jesus died on the cross for our sins and rose again. He is not dead but alive! We also believe that the only way to get to Heaven is by accepting Jesus as your Savior. What do you believe?"

"Well, like I told Aunt Joan, I accepted Jesus as my Savior.I wasn't raised going to church every Sunday. What types of programs does your church have?"

"On Sundays, Sunday school is at 9:30 A.M. at 11 A.M. is when church starts. Let my wife tell you about our weekly programs. Marie, Tiffany would like to know about our weekly programs, can you tell her."

"Okay. Sure. Well on Tuesdays during the day we have a women's group for about an hour. At night we have our music programs for the youth of our church. On Wednesday we have a community meal during the day and Bible study at night.

Thursdays we have our food pantry. Friday nights for an hour we have our youth group.

We are always looking for more volunteers."

"What kind of music lessons do you teach? Can I come to any program to just sit and watch?"

"Sure! Just let me know when. Paul tells us you are musically talented. Do you play an instrument?"

"No, I've always been interested in the piano. Singing is my thing. Maybe I can sing for you sometime."

"Well, how about you come by the church, Tuesday at 3:30? Arlene, who is our songster leader, will be there as well."

"Really? Would you give me a chance to sing at your church? But you don't know me."

"If you can keep up with Arlene, she will put you in the choir and give you a solo. This can be the start of a good friendship."

"Thank you, Marie! Can I come to church tomorrow?"

"Yes, I will introduce you to people so that way you can meet more people."

"Okay. I will be at church and see you on Tuesday at 3:30.Hey, hon, I'm going to maybe sing at Brandon's church."

"That's great! Wait! Church? Can't you sing in a bar?"

"Come on, Paul! Do this for me! It would keep me out of trouble at home.

Please?"

"Alright!"

While conversations continued, Lori continued to lose more, and more skin. Her one arm was completely wrapped in a white bandage. She hid it by wearing a hoodie even though it was summertime. Tiffany noticed and said to herself," You've messed with the wrong person."

"So, Marie, are you going to find out the sex of the baby?" Grams wanted to know.

Tiffany is angry that once again the attention is on Marie. "This is my day! Who does she think she is?" Tiffany says to herself. Tiffany pretends to be happy. Not to worry, the evil one already has Marie's demise all planned.

"Yes, Marie!" asks Tiffany. "What are your plans?"

"Well, Brandon and I just found out that I'm pregnant. We haven't had the chance to discuss any plans."

"I think you should find out, so people know what colors to get you for the baby shower."

"When we decide to, you all will know."

As the women sat on the porch talking, guys were on the back deck watching the kids and talking amongst themselves.

"So, Paul, what are your plans with this girl?" asks Brandon. "Well, I haven't thought about it. I'm just enjoying the sex."

"Are you using protection?"

"What's that?"

"Condoms!"

"Nah, I don't need them."

"You need to use them to protect you from STDs and from having children when you are not ready for them."

"What are STDs? And, I want children with Tiffany."

"STDs are sexually transmitted diseases and you shouldn't have sex until you are married."

"Oh, she doesn't have any, she would've told me. I don't believe in that sex before marriage crap anyway."

"You don't know her that well to know if she does or not. Plus, she is your first piece of ass, of course she is perfect in your eyes," comments Dan.

"Look, you guys don't know Tiffany like I do. She would never lie to me."

"How do you know? Did you check out what she's told you? Did she really lose the baby? Or where she came from? Did her parents really kick her out at 16?"

"I will prove to you Tiffany is telling the truth! I'm calling her ex. They've been together a long time."

"Well, call, but put it on speaker so we can hear," says Dan. "Hello!'

"Hey, Jose, how have you been?"

"Good. What's up?"

"I don't want to make you relive the pain of losing the baby, but did she really lose
   it?"

"Not that it's any of your business, but Tiffany didn't lose a baby because she was never pregnant."

"OMG! That is horrible lying to you like that. What do you know about her?"

"Look man, you need to watch yourself with her, she is trouble. Tiffany's family pretty much disowned her. She has
   been at Pansy House since she was 16. She still has an aunt who talks to her. She accused her dad of rape when in fact she seduced him. It tore the family up."

"WOW! She lied to me from the get go. Thanks Jose."

"Anytime. Later."

"See, we told you," Dan says.

"I know! What do I do now?"

"Confront her."

"Okay. When we get home. Aunt Joan will kick my ass if I start here."

"Yes, she will."

"So, Paul, have you guys discussed saving money for a place of your own?" asks Brandon.

"Not really. I was hoping to stay with my dad."

"Look, I know it's easy living with your dad. All you do is pay a few hundred dollars and do what you want. Your dad has a new wife, he has your grandpop to care for. With his bad heart, he doesn't need the extra stress."

"You have no business telling me to save money for my own place, when you and Marie still live with her mother."

"First off! We have our own room. We not only help pay all the bills, we help buy food, take care of the house, and help care for Grams. We don't pay $300 and lay in bed all day. There's a huge difference."

"Well, we do some work."

"From what Deb has told Joan, she comes home, and you and Tiffany are having sex. Tiffany is cleaning in the nude. Tiffany and Lori ruined dinner with a food fight. And all this in the first week you came home."

"Okay! I see your point! I never had a girlfriend; this is all new to me. Can you give me any advice?'

"Well first you need to know what you want from the relationship. Like, do you want to marriage, kids, is it just for sex?

Or do you want to just date and live together?"

"I haven't thought about any of that. I just wanna have fun."

"Then for now, saving money for a place is not a good idea. Just take things day by day for now."

"Well eventually I would like to get married and have kids. I can't say for sure if it will be with Tiffany or someone else."

"At least you are being honest."

The day is coming to an end. The women continued to sit on the porch. The men put the tables away and cleaned the floor. Both families were exhausted and said their goodbyes. The Wert household went to bed early, church tomorrow.

At the Montgomery home, Paul confronts Tiffany; Deb and Bob go to bed early. Lori continued scratching and putting on more, and more lotion.She decides to take her shower when all have gone to bed.

"Honey, what's wrong?" asks Tiffany.

"You lied to me about everything. You were never pregnant, and you were in Pansy House since 16, not on the streets like you claim. What else are you lying about?"

"Paul,why would I lie to you? I love you."

"Well, I had a nice talk with Jose. He told me everything."

"Of course, he would say I'm lying, I lost the baby and have moved on with one of his friends."

"Look, I don't care about your past. Just tell me the truth, that's all I ask."

"I promise, I will."

"Let's go to bed."

Lori unwraps her arms, her legs, skin falling off. She goes in to take a shower. She cries in pain as the water hits the already visible flesh. She tries to wash the lotion off and....

SUNDAY, AUGUST 26,1990

The water washed her remaining skin off. Her face ,her neck, every bit of skin fell off! There was nothing left, but flesh and bone. Lori became so weak she fell in the tub unconscious. All were asleep, unaware of what was going on in the bathroom.

Sunday morning! The Wert household is up getting ready for church and discussing the events from yesterday.

"So, Mom, what do you think of this Tiffany girl?" Joan asks Isabelle.

"She is a free loading whore and nothing but trouble!"

"Grams," interrupts Marie. "She's not that bad, we should give her a chance. I invited her to church."

"Well, better warn everyone to watch their wallets and the women to watch their men. She's going to rob the church and tell her boo who story to everyone."

"Mom, let's give her a chance. There's a reason God put her in our family."

"You give her a chance. I'll protect the valuables. Watch your men, ladies! The whore is here to stay."

"GRAMS!"

"What? You wait and see. I know what I'm talking about."

"Brandon, Kym, and Sam, what do you think of Tiffany?" inquires Joan.

"Well..." Brandon starts, "She's definitely different. I think she's using Bob and his family. Paul called her ex in front of Dan and I and found out she lied about a lot of stuff. I think Grams is right. We need to be careful. Something is off with this girl."

"She didn't talk to me, but from what I heard, she seems nice." adds Kym.

"I don't like her," replies Sam. "I think she's using them."

"It is our Christian duty to give this girl a chance. Remember we weren't always good people and God accepted us as we were. And that is how we are to be with others." says Marie.

"Would you like to give today's message, hon?"

"Funny!"

"Well, I think it's time to get to church. FRANKIE, LYNN, MARC! TIME TO GO! Marie, see if Celeste and Dan would come over after church for a BBQ and to go swimming."

"Sure, mom."

At the Montgomery house, everyone is just waking up. Deb goes in to take a shower....

"HELP! BOB! BOB! COME QUICK! PLEASE DON'T BE DEAD! SOMEONE HELP!

"What is it, Deb? OMG! LORI! LORI! CAN YOU HEAR ME? WHAT HAPPENED?

"I came in and found her like this."

"Deb, call 911 now!"

"911, Where is your emergency?"

"220 E. Howard street, Stowe. My...My... my sister has no skin. She's laying in the tub with nothing but flesh! Come quickly!"

"Ma'am, this is an emergency line. Every minute you waste my time, someone

dies."

"I'M TELLING THE TRUTH! I WENT TO TAKE A SHOWER AND FOUND HER IN

THE TUB WITH NO SKIN. PLEASE!!!!! SEND!!!!! HELP!!"

"I will send help. But, if this is a hoax, you will be arrested."

"FINE!!"

"What is your name?"

"Debbie Montgomery, please hurry!" "Patients name and date of birth?

"Debbie Wolfgang, 11-04-65"

"Any medical history or other symptoms?"

"Has an allergy to Levaquin, high blood pressure, a history of heart attacks, bad knees and is overweight."

"Okay, police and paramedics are on their way, stay on the line until someone comes. Is she breathing? Does she have a pulse?"

"She is barely breathing, I can't tell if there is a pulse, she has no skin!"

"Can you tell if her heart is beating?"

"It's beating very slowly."

The rest of the house goes into the bathroom to see what is going on. Kerri puts her hands over Kerreana's eyes and pushes her out. Joe laughs and says what a way to die. The others...

"Dad? What happened? Who is that?"

"Paul, we don't know what happened. This is Lori.

Trying not to laugh, Tiffany pretends to be sick.

"OMG! I'm going to throw up!"

The evil one is pleased with himself. Now, to kill the bitch off! Police and paramedics arrive, but they can only carefully take her to the hospital. Bob calls Joan to let her know what happened.

"Hey Bob, I'm at church, can I call your after?"

"Um... can someone meet us at Phoenixville Hospital? Lori was found in the shower with no skin. It doesn't look good."

good."

"OMG! What happened?"

"We don't know. Can you meet us?"

"Yes! I will be right there! Marie, Sam."

"What's up, Mom?"

"You need to get Grams and everyone home. Sam and I need to meet Bob and

Deb at Phoenixville Hospital."

"OMG! What happened?"

"Lori was found in the shower with no skin. That's all I know."

"I will tell Brandon, and we will wait to hear from you."

On the way to the hospital, Sam is told no questions. Marie fills Brandon in on what's going on. At the hospital......

"Doctor! Come quick! We have an unusual case here. A woman in her 40s, 350 pounds, has no skin. We cannot check her vitals or do any assessments."

"Put an IV in her and do a full blood panel."

"Doctor, there is no way to do anything. She has no skin; she is all flesh."

"That's impossible!"

The doctor and nurse walked into Lori's room. The nurse threw up at the sight of Lori. The doctor just stood there speechless.

"DOCTOR! Don't just stand there, help my sister!"

"Um... Can you tell me what happened? Did she take or use anything new?

"She was wearing a new lotion yesterday."

"Okay, let the police know. Unfortunately, there is nothing we can do but try and keep her comfortable."

"You're not even going to try?"

"She has no skin, so we can't run any tests or get an IV. We can try to give her something by mouth. It's a wait and see game."

"Can you do a skin graph? Or take skin from a dead person? Please! Help her!."

"She has no skin for a skin graph. And we can't use a dead person's skin. I suggest calling family and close friends to say their goodbyes."

"OH NO! Please don't die, Lori. Please!"

Devastated over the news of her sister, Deb calls up those close to her to come pay their final respects.

At church...

"Hey, Marie, we made it on time."

"Um... Tiffany! Shouldn't you both be at the hospital with Lori?"

"They said they would keep us informed."

"Okay, well you can have a seat anywhere, we are going to get started any minute."

"Good morning! It's great to be in the House of the Lord. I know we stopped opening with prayer requests, but this can't wait. A friend of ours was found this morning with no skin. She is currently at Phoenixville Hospital. My mother and Sam are there now. We will keep you informed as soon as we know more. Let's bow our heads in prayer. "

"Father,

We thank you for this beautiful day. Father, you are the great physician, healer of all things. We put our friend Lori and all needing healing in your hands. Heal their whole body. Allow them to feel your presence. Watch over who could not be here.

Father, you know the need of every prayer request on our hearts today. And we ask you to work out the situation or need today.

In Jesus' name We pray, Amen"

"We have some visitors here with us today. Please say hello. Our call to worship is Psalm 100. Helen, can you please read that for us?"

"Sure, Psalm 100

Shout for joy to the Lord, all the earth, worship the Lord with gladness Come before him with joyful songs Know that the Lord is God.

It is who made us, and we are his, we are his people, the sheep of his pasture.

Enter his gates with Thanksgiving and his courts with praise.

Give thanks to him and praise his name. For the Lord is good and his love endures forever, his faithfulness continues through all generations.

May God bless his word."

"Thank you, Helen. Arlene will be leading us in Praise and Worship."

"It's good to be in the house of the Lord this morning. OUr first song is #97, Just a closer walk with thee."

Back at the hospital, family and friends gather together to say goodbye to Lori. A nurse comes in with medicine.

"Excuse me! Nurse! What are you giving her? I thought there is nothing to help my sister?'

"The doctor ordered something to keep her comfortable."

"Thank you!"

Not too long after Lori was given the medicine, she started to go into a seizure.

Then she died. The doctor did all he could. Deb questions the doctor. Was it the medicine you gave her that caused the seizure?" "What medicine? I did not order any medicine.:

"Yes, you did!The nurse was just here 20 minutes ago. She said it was something to keep her comfortable."

"Ma'am, I'm sorry for your loss, I think you are a bit confused. We did not give her anything."

"So, you're calling me a liar? I was right here and spoke to the nurse myself."

"I'm just saying, you're confused. See here on the orders, nothing was ordered."

"But she was right here."

"I will have an autopsy ordered to see why she lost her skin and why she had the seizure. We will get to the bottom of this for you." "Thank you, doctor. Joan, can you say a prayer?"

"Sure, everyone gather around Lori and hold hands.

Father, God,

Into your hands we commit Lori's soul. Be with friends and family as we go through the grieving process. We know this is not goodbye, but see you soon.

In Jesus' name, we pray, Amen!"

"Thank you, Joan, for being here."

"It's not a problem. I'm going to call Marie and let her know."

"Hi mom, how is Lori?"

"She just passed away."

"Can I give you the details at home?"

"Sure. Hey, Tiffany and Paul are here. Shouldn't they be with Bob and Deb?'

"You would think so. Are they upset or sad?"

"No, they are calm like nothing is happening."

"That's odd. Well I need to get back to Deb."

"I'm going to tell the church."

"Okay. I love you!"

"I love you too."

"WHAT DO YOU GUYS T

-..A-

At church....

"I'm sorry to interrupt the service. I got a call from my mom, our friend Lori has gone home with the Lord. Please keep her family in praver, Okay, Arlene, you can continue."

"So sorry for your loss. Our next song is #35 Leaning on the everlasting Arms."

"Thank you, Arlene and the choir. Today's message is entitled, Spiritual cleaning."

All during church, Tiffany was smiling. One down, more to go, "This is easier than I thought it would be." Her inner demons said to themselves.

"Hi Arlene, my name is Tiffany, I'm a friend of Marie and Brandon's, I was hoping to sing with you."

"Well it's nice to meet you. But I have to discuss it with Marie, and you have to attend 4 Sundays in a row before we discuss it."

"That's not a problem."

"Hey, hon, can we go now?"

"Guess what, I'm going to be singing here."

"Wait, we have to come every Sunday?"

"Please!!! For me?"

"Can't you come yourself? Church is boring."

"Please? I will do anything you want..."

"Fine, but you owe me."

"Thank you, baby."

Both families go home to retire for the day. They all were struggling with the sudden death of Lori. She was fine and in good health.

MONDAY, AUGUST 27, 1990

Debbie hadn't slept all night. Trying to make sense of everything that happened in a short time. Her thoughts were all over. Tiffany slept like a baby. The rest of the house tossed and turned. The main bathroom is off limits until the police clear it as a crime scene.

At the Wert household, everyone was in a daze. They just saw Lori Saturday.

Joan kept thinking about the events of that day.

"Hey Marie, don't you think something was off about Lori on Saturday?"

"Like what do you mean?"

"She just didn't seem herself."

"Well, she kept putting that lotion on and remember how you kept having to bandage her arms up?"

"Yeah you're right! How did Tiffany and Paul seem at church?"

"Like nothing happened. Tiffany went and introduced herself to Arlene. And assumed she could sing in the choir. Arlene set her straight."

"Oh geez! What is this girl's deal? How was Paul?"

"Well,Paul just sat there. He didn't want to be there. That was obvious."

"Something is not right about this girl."

"Mom, she's just trying to fit in. You are reading too much into this."

"Maybe, I'm not letting my guard down."

"Okay. Do you know where Lori's services are being held?"

"No. I guess we should stop over and at least see if they need anything."

"Let me get Grams ready. She may want to come for the ride."

"Talking about me already?"

"No, Mom! We were talking about going to see how Debbie is doing and if we can help in any way. Want to come with?"

"Only if lunch is included."

"Fine, but you must behave, Mom. This is a difficult time for Debbie and her family."

Crossing her fingers, "Fine! Whatever you want."

At the Montgomery home, everyone was sad, with the exception of Paul and

Tiffany. Paul really never liked Lori. He was only nice to her because he had to be. And Tiffany, well, it's one less person she has to deal with. Tiffany decides to take a shower, which sets Debbie off.

"Where is Tiffany at, Paul?"

"I don't know! Maybe she's in the bathroom."

"There's no one in the bathroom. She better not be in the main bathroom! It can't be used."

"She could have gone for a walk to clear her head."

"True! A lot has been happening here since she's been here. I'm going to start making funeral preparations. I will be in the kitchen."

Walking past the bathroom and...

"WHAT THE HELL ARE YOU DOING?"

"WHAT THE HELL DOES IT LOOK LIKE? A SHOWER, YOU DUMB BITCH!"

"BOB! PAUL! COME GET THIS BITCH!"

"What is going on? Why all the yelling and screaming?"

"She's taking a shower in the crime scene. The police haven't even cleared it

yet!"

"Well, how the hell was I too know it's a crime scene?"

"Any idiot would know this is considered a crime scene and can't be disturbed until the police come."

"Let's all calm down, I'm sure Tiffany didn't mean to destroy evidence. Tiffany, please explain."

"First, you need to stop calling me names. Second, how was I supposed to know this is a crime scene? There was no police tape, and no one told any of us."

"Deb, I know you're hurting, but Tiffany is right. We didn't tell them to use the other bathroom."

"I'm sick and tired of you taking her side! I'm your wife or did you forget that!"

"I'm not taking her side. Look, your sister just died a horrible death. You're upset and aren't thinking clearly. Let's get some coffee and figure this out."

"NO! I don't want to figure this out. I'm fed up with Tiffany getting her own way.

Nothing she does is wrong."

"That's not true and you know it."

"What I know is my sister is dead, and Tiffany destroyed evidence, and my husband is never on my side."

"Dad, what's going on?"

"Don't worry about it, Paul."

"Fine, whatever!"

"Deb, please calm down. It will all work out!"

"I won't calm down. Just leave me alone."

As Debbie storms off to her room, Joan, Isabell, and Marie show up to talk about funeral arrangements.

"Hi all! Just wanted to stop by to see if you needed any-thing to discuss arrangements."

"Joan, I appreciate you stopping by, right now is not a good time. Deb is a mess right now. We just had a fight."

"So, where is she now?"

"In the room."

"Okay, I will talk to her."

"I apologize if she is rude or grouchy."

"Deb, it's me, Ioan. I'm here to discuss arrangements and to see how you are."

"Look, I need a day."

"I understand. But the sooner the better. The body will decay with no skin."

"Well, I'm having her cremated."

"Okay, what funeral home?"

"Um....the one on Charlotte Street."

"Okay. I will come back in a day to discuss it with you."

"Thank you, Ioan."

The police show up to do their investigation of Lori's death. Joan decides to hang out for moral support.

"Hello officer, can I help you?"

"We are looking for Debbie Montgomery."

"Yes, of course, come in. Deb... the police are here for you."

"Ma'am, my name is Officer Lamb, this is Officer Plump. We have a few questions to ask."

"Sure, this is one of my pastors, Joan Wert. I want her present.

"Do you remember anything out of the ordinary with your sister?"

"No, not that I can think of."

"If I may officer..."

"Yes, Pastor."

On Saturday, she was scratching, and I kept bandaging her arm. She kept

putting this lotion on."

"Thank you. Can we search the crime scene and her room? We also will need

that lotion."

"There is a problem with the crime scene. Someone used the shower."

"We will see what we can find."

"Okay. I will see if I can find that lotion."

Debbie goes into her sister's room where Tiffany is already going through her stuff.

Keeping what she wants.

"WHAT THE HELL ARE YOU DOING? PUT IT DOWN! YOU HAVE NO RIGHT!"

"It's not like she needs it!!"

"Why must you always start with me?"

"Look, I didn't mean to."

"I need that lotion and the business card from the salesman." Hiding the card and the lotion behind her back.

"Um...No...She used it all."

"No, she had it when we got home. What is behind your back?"

"Um..."

"Give me those! What were you going to do, destroy evidence?"

"No, I was going to give it to you. I promise."

"Yeah right! You're wasting time."

In the bathroom....

-Looks like someone tried to clean. In the drain there is something, some kind of fluid.

"Okay. Get a sample, Officer Plump."

"Did you find anything. Officer Lamb?"

"We got some samples. Is that the lotion?"

"Yes, and the business card from the person she bought it from."

"Thank you! Is there anyone you can think of that had it in for your sister?"

"NO! Everyone liked her. Wait a minute. Lori and Tiffany have been at it since

Tiffany moved in. Why would she want her dead?"

"We don't know she did."

Tiffany comes in to see what's going on.

"There she is, Officer, arrest her!"

"Arrest me for what?"

"Murder! You killed my sister! You won't get away with it. Arrest her!"

"Mrs. Montgomery, I know this is an upsetting time for you. But please let us handle this. Tiffany, I'm Officer Lamb, can I ask what your relationship was with Ms. Wolfgang?"

"Well it's no secret that we fought. But I didn't kill her. We made peace and decided to get along."

"Where were you Saturday night?"

"I was with everyone else."

"Alright! We are going to get these to the lab. Tiffany. Don't leave town."

"I won't."

"Bob, I don't want her here."

"Where am I going to go? I had nothing to do with Lori's death."

"Debbie, let's be reasonable. Where will she go?"

"She is not my problem. And if there is a chance she killed Lori, she is not welcome here. Bob, you need to support me on this."

"Sorry Paul, while Tiffany is a suspect she cannot live here."

"That's great! Where are we to go?"

"You can stay. Tiffany cannot."

"If you think I'm leaving her out on the streets in a town she doesn't know, you're fucking nuts."

"What are we going to do?"

"Let me see if the church has any funds or a place you can go. In the meantime, you can come to my place."

"Thanks, Joan."

"Sure. Debbie, when is a good time to make funeral plans?"

"Come back tomorrow at 2. Tiffany, get your shit out of my house, killer!"

"Fine, you will pay for this! Let's get our stuff."

"Hello!"

"Brandon, does the church have any housing or hotel funding?""

"No, we used it to help that homeless family. What's up?"

"Debbie kicked Tiffany out since she is a suspect in Lori's death. Paul left with her."

"Tiffany is a suspect? Why?"

"Apparently they really didn't get along. They fought a lot. Where can we put them temporarily?"

"Well we have the 2 storage rooms we can clear out for them. They cannot share a room. The church will talk."

"I agree! It's against God anyway. Let me explain the rules."

"Okay, we will clean those rooms out."

"Tiffany, Paul, the church has no funding at this time. So you will be at my house. I have some rules. You both cannot share a room or have sex at my house. I have 2 rooms you both can use. I also will not put up with the same stuff you did here. No fighting or arguing. No walking around naked or half naked. You must smoke outside. I have kids and an elderly mother. Do you both understand?"

"Yes, we understand."

"Go get your stuff. Marie, take your grandmother to the SUV. We will be out. Deb, I will see you at 2 tomorrow to make arrangements."

"Thank you for everything, Joan."

"It's not a problem."

Tiffany and Paul packed their things. The evil one is quite pleased with how well things turned out. This is going better than I planned. Now to shut this Christian family down. Who do I start with? Who...

"Where the hell do you think you're going, tramp?"

"Mom! Be nice. Paul and Tiffany will be our guests for a bit. Until her name is cleared."

"Are you crazy! She will steal everything. And what do you mean until her name is cleared. Did she kill Lori?"

"Now, Mom, she is just being asked questions. She and Lori didn't get along."

"And you want her to stay at our house? And you think I'm the mental one?"

"Grams! God would want us to help out. Tiffany, don't mind her. It's okay."

"Don't listen to me! You all will be sorry. Hide your valuables and your men!"

"It's okay. A lot of people get the wrong idea about me .Once she gets use to me, she will love me."

"The hell I will."

"Mother, that's enough! Tiffany and Paul will not be in the same bedroom. Paul's room will be the spare room off of Marc's room. And Tiffany will be in the spare room next to my room. Please be careful with PDA. You are not married and I'm teaching

Lynn to respect her body."

"Well, Paul and I are engaged, so that's like being married."

"In order to live with me, you need to respect my rules."

"Sure! No problem." (Who does that bitch think she is?) She thinks to herself.

Back at the Montgomery House..

Police were still checking the house and asking questions. All Deb kept thinking is Tiffany killed her sister, and now she's getting away with it. Her thoughts were interrupted by Officer Lamb.

"Mrs. Montgomery, we have everything we need. As soon as we have something, you will be the first to know. If you think of anything or have any questions, please don't hesitate to call."

"How could you let Tiffany get away?"

"We do not have enough evidence to arrest her. But we will look into it."

"Whatever! Are you done now?"

"We will show ourselves out. Good day."

"Deb, why don't you go lay down? You've had a hard day.'

"I don't want to. I'm tired of everybody treating me like a child and defending

Tiffany. I'm going for a drive."

"Let's talk about this." "NO,BOB! I'm done talking."

She storms out the door.

Meanwhile... At the Wert household, not everyone is happy about Joan's decisions.

"Lynn, gather everyone together for a house meeting."

"Okay, Aunt Joan."

"Well, I'm not staying. I've said what I had to say."

"Mom, please stay."

"Why? You won't listen to me anyway."

"It won't take long .I promise."

"Fine!"

"What's going on, Aunt Joan?"

"I will tell you when everyone comes down, Frankie. Okay,

Everyone, just wanted to let you all know that Tiffany and Paul will be staying with us until this investigation is over. Any questions?"

"I'm not giving up my room."

"Frankie, no one is losing their bedroom nor sharing."

"The reason the spare rooms were cleaned is for them. Paul will be sleeping in the room off of Marc's. And Tiffany will be in the room next to mine. I don't want to find out they are in each other's room. Any other questions or thoughts?"

"Aunt Joan, why do you keep taking in people? Is this a homeless shelter?"

"Lynn, the Bible says in Matthew 25:40, that whatever we do for others we do for Jesus. We are not a homeless shelter, but we are to help others less fortunate than us. This is only a temporary situation."

"Aunt Joan, what do you mean until the investigation is over?"

"Well Frankie, Tiffany is a suspect in Lori's death."

"Wait a minute! Tiffany may have killed Lori and you are moving her in? Does the Bible say to put your family in danger to help others?"

"No, but she has not been convicted, there is no evidence that she did anything. They are just asking questions. Frankie, the Bible teaches us to be careful, to not judge, to forgive."

"Well I'm getting a lock for my door. Marc, hide your valuables."

"What are you saying, Frankie, that my girl and I steal?"

"Yes, I am. Come on Paul, you know you've stolen from Mom and me. And no one knows this girl you forced on everyone. Let's face it, you're with her because she looks like Marie."

"If that's how you feel, Frankie, let's take this outside."

"Let's go!"

"ENOUGH! Frankie, Paul, calm down and think this through. Your aunt is trying to help and since we live with her, we need to respect her decisions."

"Brandon is right! Let's calm down and figure all this out."

"Marie, I'm sorry but it had to be said."

"It's okay, Frankie. I'm not even worried about it."

"To clear the air, I don't steal and I'm not with Tiffany because she looks like Marie. I'm done with all that. Thank you, Aunt Joan for taking us in."

"Well, I have something to say."

"Please! Not now, Mom."

"Everyone else had their say, why can't I?"

"Fine!"

"Everyone needs to be careful. This girl is pure evil. No one is safe."

"Okay, Mom, Time for your medication."

"I'm not crazy! I know more than you think I do.""

"Anything else? Okay, let's get them settled in and enjoy our evening."

The rest of the evening, the Wert household discussed amongst themselves the new addition to their household. Frankie is pissed that his aunt keeps taking people in. Marc is new to this whole family thing. Brandon and Marie are just hoping that Joan is careful. Sam and Kym don't care. Scott wishes he had his own place. Lynn hopes they don't stay long. And Grams sees right through Tiffany's act. She knows there is something wrong with this girl.

At the Montgomery house, Bob and Deb slept in separate bedrooms. Kerri took Kerrena to a hotel for a while.

What happened to their aunt has haunted Kerri ever since. She doesn't know if she can ever go back. The house had an eerie silence.

Bob tried talking to Deb, but she ignored him. His dad was sleeping like a baby.

TUESDAY, AUGUST 28,1990

It's a beautiful Tuesday morning. The sun is out, the birds are singing. Tiffany is up early. Hoping to get Paul alone before anyone gets up. But her plans are ruined. Joan, Brandon ,Marie, and Isabelle are all up and making breakfast for all, discussing their plans for the day.

"So, Mom, what are your plans for today?"

"Well, I was going to ask Brandon if he would come with me to Deb's to get funeral plans ready. How about you?"

"I have to meet Arlene about this week's programs and thought I would show Tiffany around town. How about coming with Grams? I will buy lunch at your favorite place."

"The Very Best? Does she have to come?"

"I just thought it would be nice to show Tiffany around Pottstown. It will be fun!" "Fine! I will go."

"Is that okay with you, Tiffany?'

"Can Paul come with?"

"How about it just be us? I don't want to take a lot of people to Arlene's"

"Okay, let me get dressed. Is Paul up yet?"

"I'm not sure, he went to bed early. He's upset that Deb put you out and is accusing you of murder."

"Can I go talk to him?"

"You can when he comes down. Marc is still sleeping."

"Paul and I shouldn't have to live like this. We are engaged. That means married."

"If you don't like the rules here, you can leave. And being engaged does not mean married. Give me your answer before you leave."

"Well I have no other place to go.I will follow your rules."(The evil one already has a plan for her to be with Paul regardless of the rules.)

"Good to hear. Well, I need to get ready to go. We need to leave at about
9:30."

"No problem!"

"Grams! Tiffany! We need to get going. Arlene is expecting us."

At the Montgomery house, things were tense. Bob tries to apologize, but Deb is still angry at him and only wants to focus on the services for Lori.

"Deb, can we talk?"

"I have nothing to say to you. Everything is Tiffany. So talk to her."

"Come on! I said I was sorry."

"Now you're sorry? You weren't sorry when she walked around naked, when I walked in the house to find them having sex, or when she had a food fight ruining dinner. But, now that she killed Lori, now you're sorry! Well it's a little too late. Tiffany already killed someone."

"Deb, there is no evidence that she killed Lori. And all I wanted to do was give Tiffany a chance. She did not grow up in the structured family setting we have. You have to expect her to test the waters."

"Bob, I don't want to discuss this with you anymore. Joan will be here soon to go over Lori's service. I don't want her in the middle of us fighting."

"Can't we just sit and talk until Joan comes?"

"NO! Now I need to get ready."

"Deb, I love you! And will be here for you."

"Well you're too late. Joan and Brandon are here."

"Hi Deb, is this a good time?"

"Yes. Sorry for the mess. Would you and Brandon like something to drink?"

"We are good. Thank you."

"You can sit here."

"Have you thought about the service for Lori?"

"Honestly, Joan, Bob and I have been arguing. I haven't had a moment to think about anything."

"Okay, so why don't we start with the songs. What are her favorite songs?"

"Um... The Old Rugged Cross, Victory in Jesus and In Christ alone."

"Well, this is a good start. Can I add some songs?"

"Sure, whatever you think is best."

"Does she have any favorite passages of scripture?"

"Truthfully, I don't know. Can you just put something together?"

"Sure. Is this Saturday good to have her funeral?"

"Yeah ,the sooner the better."

"Good. Say 10 for a viewing of pictures and things you would like to show. And the services can start at about 11.Do you want a reception afterwards?"

"NO! Are we done?"

"Uh... Yeah! On Friday I will show you the outline for the service. And I will make all the arrangements with the funeral home."

"Sounds good to me."

"Great! Brandon, can you please pray?"

"Sure, Father, we ask that you comfort Bob and Deb in their time of mourning.

Allow them to feel your love and arms around them. In Jesus' name, Amen."

"Brandon, can I speak with you for a moment?"

"Sure, what's up?"

"Can Deb and I come in for therapy?"

"Are you both doing okay?"

"Ever since Tiffany came, no. Deb thinks I take Tiffany's side in everything."

"I see. Let's talk about this more after Lori's funeral. Give Deb some time to process everything."

"Okay, thank you."

At the Wert household, Paul, Marc, and Frankie are just playing video games.

The ladies...

"Hi, Arlene, I hope you don't mind the extras. We have some errands to run

after I leave."

"It's not a problem. Come in, have a seat. Would you like anything to drink?"

"No, thank you! We are good."

"Hi, Arlene! Remember me?"

"Um...yes! Tiffany, right?"

"Yes. Can you hear me sing today? I'd love to sing with your choir."

"Marie, will you please explain to Tiffany how things work?"

"Tiffany, first you have to attend 4 Sundays in a row. Then Arlene can listen to you sing. And then the leaders of the church can vote you in. But you still need to attend regularly."

"Arlene, watch her. She is the devil!"

"Grams! You promised to behave! I'm sorry, Arlene. Grams, for whatever reason, does not like Tiffany."

"Mark my words, she is the devil!"

"Grams, we will discuss this later."

"Arlene, let's get started on this week's program. Grams, be nice. Lynn let me know if Grams starts."

"Okay ,Marie."

"Don't worry, Marle, we will be okay."

As Tiffany puts on a fake smile, the evil one begins to plan the murder of Grams. She picked the wrong one. I will take over this family and will destroy their church, starting with the choir.

Her thoughts were interrupted by Lynn asking a question.

"Tiffany, can you play a game with me?"

"Sure, sweetie. What would you like to play?"

"War."

"Go get the cards."

"Leave her alone!"

Tiffany goes up to Grams and gives her a sinister look with glowing red eyes.

Grams is not intimidated.

"You don't scare me, Satan!"

Grams begins to yell. Marie and Arlene run in to see what is going on.

"What is going on?"

"She yelled at me and called me Satan! I just wanted to apologize."

"Grams!"

"She gave me the devil's look with red eyes."

"Lynn, what happened?"

"I don't know, I went to get the cards and came back to this."

"Okay, I've had enough! You both owe Arlene an apology. I am very sorry."

"It's okay. I will email you my stuff for programs and Sunday."

"Okay, thank you. Let's go."

"Marie, I'm hungry."

"Well, I should go straight home, but I need to feed Lynn.But you both need to be on your best behavior."

"Okay, I will behave."

"Good."

At the police station.....

"Detective Lamb, what do you think about this case?"

"We don't have a lot to go on. Hopefully we get lucky and get a fingerprint off that card. Any word back from the crime lab?"

"I can call down."

"Yeah, do that. When you're done see if there have been other unusual deaths or murders surrounding Miss Powers."

"How far back should I go?"

"At least 5 years."

"Will do."

As they get started into the investigation, the crime lab tech and the corner come in to give their findings."

"Larry, Mel, any findings?"

"Well, there were 4 sets of prints, the victim's, Tiffany Powers, Paul Montgomery, and an odd set of prints. A 666 print."

"You mean someone wrote 666 on their fingerprint and it showed on the card?"

"No, the fingerprint is 666. I also found boric acid in the lotion."

"Boric acid? The stuff that kills roaches?"

"Typically, yes. In large quantities it can eat human skin."

"Do you have the cause of death, Mel?"

"Yes! I found high quantities of acid in her flesh. She had an allergic reaction to an antibiotic called Levaquin, which killed her."

"That body lotion is not big enough for large amounts of boric acid."

"If she kept reapplying it, that could be enough to put large amounts in her system to take her skin off."

"Okay, thank you."

"Detective Plumb, narrow your search to crimes with 666 fingerprints. I have to ask the sister a few more questions."

During Detective Plumb's search, he came across the 2 murders at Pansy House, while Detective Lamb brings in Deb for more questions.

"There were 2 mysterious deaths at a place called Pansy House in Bryn Mawr just recently. A fan fell on a teenager and the other was a therapist who drank something with acid and all that was left was her organs. The fingerprints for both were 666. Here is the best part, Tiffany Powers and Paul Montgomery were at Pansy House at the time of the murders. Tiffany was the main suspect of the young girl's death, but her alibi was solid."

"Wow! Maybe we need to bring them both in for more questions. Here comes

Mrs. Montgomery. Get copies of both investigations."

"Okay, I will."

"Mrs. Montgomery, have a seat. Would you like something to drink?"

"Let's get this over with!"

"Right! Let's start with the lotion. Were you home or with the victim when she bought the lotion?"

"Her name is Lori, not the victim! I was not home or with when she bought it. She said a man came to the house."

"Did she only put it on once?"

"I don't know. The day we were at our pastor's house,every time she itched she kept putting more on. Come to think of it, we had to keep bandaging her up."

"Okay. What can you tell me about Tiffany Powers?"

"Is she a suspect?"

"I can't say right now. Just need more information."

"Well I don't know much about her. She was put out at an early age and went to

Pansy House. That is where Paul met her."

"So Paul met her and that's how you met her?"

"Yes."

"Do you know anything about the Pansy House murders?"

"All I know is because of the murders, Pansy House closed.

We were not given any details."

"Okay. Did Lori have any allergies?"

"Yes, to Levaquin."

"Thank you for your time. That's all the questions I have for now."

"As soon as you know something, please let me know."

"Yes, of course. Just know we are treating this as a homicide."

"OH! Thank you!"

At the Montgomery house, Deb still refuses to talk to Bob.They slept in separate rooms.

At the Wert house, Marie was still upset over Gram's behavior. She told her mom and Brandon about it as they were going over the service for Lori. Grams prayed for protection against the evil one. Tiffany was quite pleased with herself. The evil one already was planning on how to get rid of Grams.

All retire for the evening. Tomorrow is a new day.

WEDNESDAY, AUGUST 29,1990

Deb woke up in a good mood, until Bob comes into the room.

"Deb! Can we please talk?"

"What is there to talk about? You will never see it my way."

"It's not about seeing it one way or the other. We can't go on ignoring each other or arguing."

"Look, ever since Tiffany got here, you take her side in everything. You promised me that if she causes any trouble, she goes. She has caused so much trouble and each time you made an excuse. Now she is gone, now I'm good enough."

"Deb, it's a big adjustment living in a new place, new rules. A place where you don't know anyone."

"I get all that to a point. You allowed this girl to do whatever she wanted. She walked around naked, had sex all day, had a food fight. Then she killed my sister. And now you want to talk? It's too damn late to say sorry."

"Come on, Deb. Be reasonable. Why can't we work this out?"

"You allowed a killer in the house and Lori is gone. What is there to work out? Tell me!"

"I'm sorry I didn't listen to you. You cannot honestly expect me to know that Tiffany would be a suspect in a murder case. Or do any of the things she did here."

"I just need some space, Bob. I'm tired of arguing with you. Let's just drop it. It seems like Tiffany is the main suspect. Detective Lamb called me in for more questions."

"Why didn't you tell me? Why won't you let me be here for you?"

"I just lost my sister and you kept defending Tiffany. But I'm ready to let you be here for me."

"Thank you."

At the Wert house, things are a bit rocky. Tiffany tries to be nice, but Grams is not having it. Marie makes plans with her cousin, Celeste. Joan and Brandon get things together for Lori's service. Paul tries to connect with Frankie and Marc with little luck.

The roommate Scott watches a movie with Lynn.

"Morning, Isabell, would you like something to eat and drink?"

"Where is my daughter?"

"I think she and Brandon are at the church."

"Fine! I will wait for Marie or someone else."

"Look, I'm trying to be nice and to fit in. Why are you making things so difficult for me? I've done nothing to you."

"I see right through you. You are the devil, out to destroy everyone and everything. You can't get anything past me."

"Watch yourself, old woman. You have no idea who you are messing with."

"What's going on?"

"Grams and I were just getting better acquainted. Would you like some breakfast, Marie?"

"I'm just getting coffee. Celeste and I are meeting at Friendly's for breakfast. Then off to our doctor's appointments. And probably some shopping."

"Isn't that nice, Gram?"

"DON'T CALL ME GRAMS! Who will be here with me?"

"Scott, the boys, Lynn, and Tiffany."

"Great! Can I come with you?"

"Grams, I just need some me time. I'm still upset over yesterday."

"I understand. I'm not sorry. I met every word I said!"

"I'm off. Please behave. Scott, call me if there are any problems."

"Will do. Oh, are there any chores that need to be done?"

"Just clean up after yourselves. Alright, I'm leaving." After a few hours, Frankie comes downstairs.

"Hey Grams, where is everyone?"

"Hi Frankie, Marc and Paul are still sleeping. Your aunt and Brandon are at church with Arlene getting ready for Lori's service. Marie is meeting Celeste and everyone else is here. What are your plans for today?"

"Marc and I are playing games. How about we bring our systems down and sit with you? I don't want you alone with that girl."

"Thank you, Frankie. I appreciate it."

"Love you, Grams!"

"Love you, too!"

Paul and Tiffany came down.

"Hey Frankie, can I hang out with you and Marc today?"

"No! Paul, you are spending the day with me."

"Why can't I spend time with my family?"

"Because I'm your fiancée and Marie didn't get to show me around yesterday so you can?"

"Can't we do it another day? I don't get to see Frankie, he goes to school."

"No! You are spending time with me, since we can't sleep together living here."

"Fine! Whatever!"

"Come on, let's go."

Celeste and Marie enjoy their breakfast and head to their doctor's appointments before going shopping for baby stuff.

Their doctor, Dr. Oreo, gives some exciting news.

"Alright ladies, who wants to go first?"

"Since it's Marie's first pregnancy, let her go first."

"Okay, Marie, this will be warm, you will feel some pressure. There are 2 sets of fingers, toes, feet, legs, and arms. There is a mouth, nose, 2 eyes and ears, a head, and the whole body. Everything looks good. I can see the sex.... would you like to know what you are having?"

"Congratulations! You are having a girl! Here is a picture of your ultrasound. There is a bathroom on your right for you to get cleaned up and change in. Okay, Celeste, you're next."

"You don't have to go through the details unless there is a problem."

"Sounds good. Everything is all there and looks good. Do you want to know the sex?"

"YES!"

"Congratulations! You are having a girl!"

"REALLY?"

"Yes, see for yourself."

"I always wanted a girl."

"Well, now you have one of each. Go share the news with your cousin."

"So, how was your first ultrasound?"

"Well, the doctor says everything looks good. And.... I'm having a girl!"

"Really!!! So am I."

"Yay! They will grow up being best friends. I'm so excited.I can't wait to tell

Brandon."

"Come on, let's do some shopping."

"Hey....maybe we can tell the family together at a family dinner."

"That sounds good. When? This Saturday is Lori's funeral."

"How about next Saturday? I can make that chicken pasta dish and my biscuits, and you can make dessert."

"Girl, I can't bake. You mean I can buy dessert."

"Yeah, I forgot. I will run it by my mom tomorrow."

Marie and Celeste do some shopping and then head home to see their husbands. At the Wert house everyone retires for the day to enjoy a good night's sleep.

At the Montgomery house, Bob and Deb watch movies together before going to bed for the night.

THURSDAY, AUGUST 30,1990

Bob and Deb got up early, went for breakfast before they started to go through and pack up Lori's stuff. People kept calling and stopping by offering their condolences. Deb tried thinking of the good memories. But all she could think about was how much Lori and Tiffany fought.

The Wert household was up and moving. Today was food pantry day at the church. Tiffany talks Paul into volunteering. Marc, Lynn, and Frankie are at school. Marie talks to her mom about having a family dinner.

"Morning, Mom. Before we go to church, can we talk?"

"Sure, what's up?"

"Celeste and I found out the sex of our babies yesterday. We wanted to know if next Saturday we could have a family dinner to announce the sex?"

"You mean like a baby shower?"

"Isn't it too soon?"

"You are farther along than we thought."

"How long did the doctor say you were?"

"He said 6 months for us both."

"We can have one for you and Celeste at the same time. You and Celeste give me a list of people to invite and the addresses. We can have it at the church."

"Are you sure, Mom?"

"Yes! It may be short notice, but we can make it work."

"I will let Celeste know at church today."

"Great! I need to send out the invitations by Saturday."

"Mom, it would be easier to put it on social media. Post as a private event and invite who you want."

"Sounds good."

Isabelle, Paul, and Tiffany join them for breakfast. And ask what the plans are for the day.

"Morning! What's up for today?"

"Well today is food pantry day; would you like to join us, Tiffany?"

"Can we, Paul?"

"Why can't I just stay home, and you go?"

"Because I don't know anyone, PLEASE?"

"FINE! But you owe me big!"

"Thank you!"

"Are you helping today, Mom?"

"Of course! Gotta keep my eye on her. No one is safe around her."

"Already this morning. Just give her a chance."

"Why should I?"

"Mom, I hope you can behave at the funeral on Saturday. Oh, and next Saturday we are having a baby shower for Marie and Celeste."

"How nice. Is the devil invited?"

"Look here, old woman! I had enough of your name calling. Back off or else!"

"Or else what? Bring it! I'm not afraid of you."

"ENOUGH! BOTH OF YOU!"

-If you both can't get along then at least be quiet. NO one wants to hear it."

The evil one begins to think of a way to get rid of Isabell. She's on to us already! Need to take her out! "Correction, she's only on to you," Liar says to the evil one. "Well, I will deal with her

personally."

"I will be nice if Isabell stops calling me the devil."

"Just stay out of my way and everything will be fine."

"Okay!"

"Mom, Grams can ride with me, and Tiffany and Paul can go with you."

"What about Sam and Kym?"

"I forgot about them. They can come with me."

"Paul, can you let your mom and Sam know we are leaving?"

"Sure, Aunt Joan."

"Sam and Kym, came down." Sam complains about everything as always.

Kym just keeps playing with her phone.

"It's too early to be up."

"Today is food pantry day. So let's get moving. You and Kym will go with

Marie. Tiffany and Paul will ride with me."

"Why can't we ride with you?"

"Because Kym is too big for my Nissan."

"Alright! Let me get my soda and snack bag. What are you going to have them do?"

"Don't worry about it! Let's get going."

At the food pantry, everyone gets to work right away. Celeste and Marie write out their invitation lists. Their church served 100 families. Afterwards, Joan had Frankie pick up Marc and Lynn and meet them at Friendly's for dinner. At dinner, Isabell tries to get information about the sex of Marie's baby. Sam tries to get more information out of Tiffany about herself. Marc and Frankie were playing on their phones. Lynn wanted to know about the babies.

"So, Marie, did you find out the sex of the baby?"

"Celeste and I both found out. That's why we are having a baby shower together. "I'm sorry, Celeste, I forgot you were pregnant, too."

"It's okay, Grams. This is Marie's first, she should get the attention."

"Grams, all I can say is Celeste and I are having the same sex."

"Just give me a hint. Like what color scheme? Dresses or pants?"

"Grams, not until the shower."

"Tiffany, do you have any children?"

"No, Sam, I don't. Remember, I had a miscarriage."

"Oh, that's right."

"Tell the truth! You weren't pregnant. Jose told me the truth."

"Stay out of my conversation, Paul!"

"Stop lying to my family."

"I'm not!"

"Whatever!"

"Guys! We are in a restaurant."

"Sorry, Aunt Joan."

"Do you plan on marrying Paul, Tiffany?"

"I'd like to when I am ready."

"It's none of your business, Sam."

"I'm trying to make conversation."

"Haven't you asked enough questions tonight?"

"It's okay, Paul. Damn, all you need to know is I love Paul, we are together. If we get married, we get married. If not, then no."

"Are you done now?"

"Yes!"

"Good! Let's get back to the baby."

"Grams!"

"WHAT! It's your first baby, the focus should be on you, not her.

Tiffany is getting angry. The evil one has a plan to deal with this. But, first things first, get rid of the old woman before the rest believe her.

The rest of dinner went well. Celeste and Marie handed Joan their invite list for the baby shower. Tiffany is so angry she decides to ruin the baby shower. What she doesn't know is Joan has it all planned. All she needs to do is set the date. And all the information is on the church computer she uses. She doesn't want anyone accessing the plans and telling Marie or Celeste.

The Wert family had a long day. As soon as they got home,they all went to their rooms. Tiffany tried sneaking off to Paul's room. But her plans failed.

"Paul! Wait up."

"Tiffany, if my aunt finds out she will kick us out."

"She will never know."

"I have to go through Marc's room to get to my room."

"Don't worry about him. He's so busy playing video games, he will never know.

And if he does see me, he won't say a word."

"Tiffany, we need to respect my aunt."

"Paul, I am your soon to be wife. Be more concerned with making me happy."

"Keep your voice down, Tiffany."

"I don't care who hears me. I will say what I want."

"What is going on here? People are trying to relax for the night."

"Why can't we be in each other's rooms and spend time together?"

"I do not believe in sex before marriage. You don't have to live here. If you can't respect my rules, then leave."

"Aunt Joan, we will respect your rules. Right, Tiffany?"

"Alright, see you guys tomorrow."

"Why couldn't you stand up to her? Don't you love me?"

"I do love you. But I will always respect my aunt Joan. If you can't handle that, then we are over."

"Paul, come on."

"I mean it, Tiffany."

"Okay."

All of a sudden, laughter and yelling came from nowhere. It's Grams.

"Alright! Tell her like it is, Paul. Kick her to the streets."

"Grams, you're not helping."

"Can't get rid of me that fast."

"It's time to show her who is in charge here. It is me." Tiffany thinks to herself. I will get even with that old bat. As Tiffany walks past Grams's room, she sees a box of funnel cake sitting on the dresser. A thought immediately came to mind. The rest of the evening was quiet and peaceful. Tiffany was busy looking up the stuff she needed to follow through with the evil one's plan.

The Montgomery's went to bed early. They had a busy day. One day before Lori's funeral. Deb was going through a lot of emotions. Packing her sister's stuff was not an easy task. She wishes she could keep it all. She kept some items. Tomorrow she will go over the final funeral arrangements. And call Detective Lamb about her sister's case.

FRIDAY, AUGUST 31, 1990

It's the day before Lori's funeral. Joan needed to go to Deb's and go through everything. Deb had plans on talking to Detective Lamb on if they have any new developments. Tiffany needed to figure out how to sneak her supplies in the house. "Good morning, Mom. What are your plans for today?"

"Well, Brandon and I are meeting with Deb to go over things for tomorrow. Want to come with?"

"No, I thought I would invite Celeste over to have a girls 'day. Maybe have Grams and Lynn come with. Can you invite Deb for me?"

"Deb? Are you sure?"

"She needs to be around people at this time. She is in a way family."

"Yeah, you're right."

"Good morning! What is up for today?"

"I'm going to Deb's and Marie is hanging with Celeste. What are you and Paul doing today?"

"He is taking me to the mall to hang with some friends of his."

"Have fun."

"Does anyone have any money I can borrow to get something to eat or drink? I can pay it back when my check comes."

"Here is $50. You don't have to pay me back."

"Thank you, Marie."

"Not a problem. Morning, Grams! Do you have plans to-day?"

"I want to relax?"

"I thought you and Lynn would want to have a girls' day with me and Celeste."

"Doing what? And, is food involved?"

"We can go shopping and out to eat."

"Well, if you're paying, count me in."

"Yes, I am paying."

"Can you go get Brandon, Marie?"

"Here he comes now."

"Well, we are off."

At the Montgomery house, Deb is on the phone with Detective Lamb, as Bob is getting ready for Joan and Brandon to come.

"Pottstown Police Department, Detective Lamb speaking, how can I help you?"

"This is Deb Montgomery, I was wondering if there are any leads in my sister's case?"

"Mrs. Montgomery, if anything new comes up, you will be the first person I call. I promise."

"I'm just wondering how Tiffany is free! Why wasn't she arrested?"

"Because there is not enough evidence to arrest her."

"Great! So until then she is free to do what she wants, to kill her next victim!"

"Just because they didn't get along, doesn't mean she killed her."

"Well, I know in my heart she did. I won't rest until she is stopped."

"Please let us handle it. Promise me you won't take the law into your own hands?"

"Oh, I won't have to. She will mess up sometime."

"Deb! Joan and Brandon are here."

"Okay, I will be down in a minute."

"Come in and have a seat. Would you like something to drink?"

<

--

"I would like some tea, what about you Brandon?"

"Nothing for me."

"Okay, I will be right back."

"Hi guys! I was on the phone with Detective Lamb."

"Any new leads?"

"Well you know how it goes, Joan, they need evidence to arrest Tiffany."

"Tiffany? They feel she did it?"

"No, they don't, but I am sure it was her."

"Okay, well, there is still lots to do for tomorrow. So, let's get through what we have outlined.

Preliminary music-Wendy Sheets

Welcome-Marie Kwon

Song-In Christ Alone (Arlene Gebhard)

Tribute from friends

Solo-Arlene Gebhard

Tribute from friends

Old Testament reading- Psalm 90:1-6,10,12,14,16,17 Joan Wert

Tribute from friends

New Testament reading-John 14:16 Isabell Wert

Meditation-Pastor Kwon

Song-I'll Go in the Strength of the Lord Arlene Gebhard

Benediction-Joan Wert

"It looks good. Thank you for putting this all together for me."

"It's not a problem. We will arrange the flowers so it doesn't look crowded. Did you put together pictures so people can look at them? Like a memorial." "I will work on it today. What time would you like us there?"

"Come about 8:00 A.M. That way last minute stuff can get done."

"Sounds good. I really hope Tiffany doesn't show up."

"Paul won't go without her."

"I just don't want drama or problems."

"I can understand that. Maybe she will be on her best behavior."

"Joan, this girl is nothing but trouble. Before I forget, can you give them their checks? They came here."

"Sure, I will make sure they get them. I am having a baby shower for Marie and Celeste next Saturday; we are hoping you will join us."

"Thank you both, I will think about it. Well, I need to get started on the memory board. We will see you tomorrow."

"We will see you tomorrow."

"Okay. See you then."

Back at the Wert house, Celeste and Marie were having fun hanging out with Grams and Lynn. When Tiffany and Paul came in.

"Hey guys, what are you up to?"

"Just hanging out. Having a girls' day. Would you like to come to our baby shower?"

"Really? I would love to. For a girl or boy?"

"We will announce it at the shower."

"Thank you. When is it?"

"You will have to ask my mom."

"Okay, I will."

"So, did you guys have fun at the mall?"

"It was okay. I thought it was boring. I'm used to a lot of stores, crowds of people. This mall has nothing of interest."

"Well, it has the interest of the local teens. What things do you think every mall should have?"

"Things like sexy clothes, baby store, toys, different cultures of food and stuff."

"Okay. How do you like Paul's friends?"

"They are too childish and goofy."

"You know for someone who doesn't have friends outside of family, you sure are picky and judgmental."

"I'm not being picky and judgmental, Celeste. I just don't want to hang out with children. They need to grow up. Paul's friends made farting noises and they played with their food. They were too goofy."

"They still make farting noises?"

"Yes! Especially when people walk by."

"OH, wow!"

"I need to get going, Marie. Can you give this to your mom?"

"Sure, Celeste. I had fun. Give JR a hug and kiss for me."

"I will. Grams, behave."

"That's no fun."

"Okay, bye."

At dinner, Grams just wanted to talk about the baby shower. She knew talking about the pregnancy irritated Tiffany. But she didn't care.

"Have you sent the invitations out yet, Joan?"

"Well I am using social media and for the people at church there will be an announcement on Sunday."

"What colors are you doing, and what all is planned?"

"The colors are pink and blue. There will be catered food, the cake is ordered. We are playing games like guessing the sex ,and how big the belly is. We are going to have lots of fun. "Isn't it too late for catered food?"

"No, Mom! I already had everything planned. I just need the number of people and the date."

"When is it?"

"Next Saturday."

"That's not a lot of time. Are you sure it's enough notice, Joan?"

"I know it's short notice but the sooner the better. Then we can focus on what we need yet and get the room ready. Would you like to help me, Mom?"

"Yes!"

"Can I help, Joan?"

"You can help with some stuff."

"Don't let that devil help! Hell, don't even invite her."

"Stop calling me names! I am not the devil. Why can't I come and help?"

"Alright that's enough. Of course, you can help and come."

"Who does this bitch think she is?" The evil one vents to the liar and manipulator.

"We need to get rid of her before they start believing her."

"Thank you, Joan."

"You're welcome. Marc and Frankie, you have dishes. Brandon and Marie, you can clear the table."

After dinner, everyone went up to their rooms for the night. Tomorrow is Lori's funeral. Marie is worried about Deb's reaction if Tiffany shows. Tiffany can't wait to get rid of Grams. She also wished there was something she could do to Marie. Everything revolves around Marie because she is pregnant.

SATURDAY, SEPTEMBER 1,1990

It is the day of the funeral. Deb and Bob got the memory boards and headed to the church. The Wert household was up and getting ready to go. Of course, Grams has to start with Tiffany.

"Morning everyone. Can we get a ride with someone to the service?"

"Who said you can go? No one wants you there, especially when you are a suspect."

"I did not kill Lori. We had our differences, but we made amends."

"Yeah right! You will say anything to get the suspicion off you."

"Both of you, cool it! Today is not the day for arguing. We are all going to be on our best behavior. Deb does not need this. She needs all the support she can get."

"Fine! For Deb, and today only, I will be nice. But I will be watching you."

"Mom, stop! Mom and Lynn can ride with Brandon and Marie .Tiffany ,Paul, and the boys can ride with me."

As soon as they get to the church, there is some chaos. Deb is really not happy Tiffany showed up.

"How dare you show up here today!"

"Deb, I'm not trying to start anything, I just want to pay my respects."

"Look, this is not the time for this. People will be showing up soon. I will keep an eye on Tiffany. Now let's get ready for people to come. Tiffany, can you set up that table with the sign

In books and programs? Brandon and Frankle, get the sound board and computer working. Mare and Paul can set up some extra chairs. Mom, help Deb get the flowers and memory boards up. Lynn, put a pack of tissues at each seat."

"Brandon, can you put these pics on the screen?"

"Sure. How are things going on with you and Deb?"

"We had a talk and are trying to work things out."

"That's great!"

"But I still feel like we need to come in for counseling. We still have problems."

"Okay, well, when both of you are ready, just give me a call."

"We will,"

People start coming in and shortly after the service starts. The preliminary music is played by Wendy Sheetz. She played Amazing Grace.

"Good morning everyone. Sorry we have to meet under these circumstances. I am Marie Kwon, one of the pastors here. Arlene will be leading our songs. Our first song is In Christ Alone. The words are on the program."

"If anyone has a memory they would like to share, please stand up."

"My name is Isabell Wert. Lori loved nice smelling lotion. We would always share the new lotions we got."

"Thank you for sharing."

"My name is Tom. Lori and I used to work together. She always was in a positive mood. One time I was having a rough day. She tried to cheer me up. I am grateful to have met Lori."

"Thank you for sharing. Anyone else? Arlene will be singing a solo called, "We shall Behold Him, a Sandi Patti song."

"Would anyone else like to share anything?"

All were quiet; no one stood up.

"Joan will be reading from the Old Testament."

"Does anyone have a memory they would like to share?"

"My name is Tiffany. Lori and I didn't always get along..."

"HOW DARE YOU! TRYING TO ACT LIKE YOU BOTH WERE FRIENDS!"

"Deb, let's not make a scene."

"I'M TIRED OF EVERYONE DEFENDING HER. SHE KILLED MY SISTER!"

"Deb, calm down. No one is defending her. Everyone is here to honor Lori. This is not honoring Lori."

"ALRIGHT!"

"I think memory sharing time is over. Isabell will be reading from the New

Testament."

"Before I begin, Tiffany Powers is the devil! Everyone be careful, watch your..."

"Mom! This is not the time nor the place. Have a seat."

The evil one is pissed! She goes this weekend!

"I want to apologize for the outbursts. I think we should sing the last song, "I'll Go in the Strength of the Lord.""

"Everyone feel free to look at the pictures and come downstairs for a snack."

"Grams! What in the world were you thinking?"

"People should know to stay away from Tiffany. You mark my words, that girl is evil. I bet she is planning her next murder."

"Grams! This is a funeral. You helped ruin Lori's service. This service was to honor a good woman, and you turned it into a witch hunt for your craziness. Go and apologize to Deb."

"I will not! Deb started it all!"

"And you just had to add your 2 cents in!"

"I did nothing wrong! But I will apologize to Debi will not apologize to Tiffany!"

"Whatever! I have nothing more to say to you."

Tiffany overheard everything. How does this old woman know we are evil? She needs to go A.S.A.P. Before everything is ruined and they start to listen to her. The perfect time to handle this is on... Their thoughts were interrupted by Joan.

"Tiffany, I am sorry for Deb and my mother. This was not the place. Deb should have let you share."

"It's not your fault. I don't think they will ever like me."

"Just give it some time."

"Okay."

Deb is still angry with Tiffany. She goes to confront her when she is interrupted.

"Deb! Sorry for how things went. Are you alright?"

"I was trying to get to Tiffany. I have a few words to say to her."

"Do you think that is a wise decision?"

"Yes, I do, Joan. Once again she ruins everything."

"You and my mother did that. She barely said anything. Look, I know you don't like her, you think she killed your sister. But you have to drop this. It's not healthy. Do you think Lori would want you to be bitter?"

"I don't care! I will leave it alone for today only! For my sister."

"Thank you."

The rest of the day went smoothly. Everyone sat and reminisced about Lori. Bob and Deb stayed to help clean up. Every-one was so tired that when they got home, they went straight to their rooms. All Tiffany could think about was getting rid of Grams. The switch of the funnel cakes will be Sunday when they are at church. She can't wait.

Now, to plan her next mission. This one was top secret.

Deb and Bob went straight to bed. They were exhausted. Tomorrow is a new day.

SUNDAY SEPTEMBER 2,1990

The Wert family was still tired from yesterday. Grams couldn't wait to talk with Arlene. Joan wanted to get in early to use her computer there to finalize the plans and get everything set on social media. Frankie and Marc did not want to go. Tiffany played sick.

"Morning, everyone! I need to get to the church early, so whoever is riding with me, let's go."

"Aunt Joan, can Marc and I stay home?"

"Are you sick?"

"No."

"Then no. Kym and Sam, who are you riding with?"

"We will ride with you."

"Tiffany and mom?"

"I'm riding with you."

"Tiffany?"

"I'm not feeling good. I'm just going to sleep."

"Okay, well Scott is here so if you need anything."

"Okay."

"Boys! Get ready."

"Morning, Mom!"

"I'm going in early, Marie. The boys are coming with you and Brandon, Tiffany is staying home."

"Okay. We are leaving in a few."

"Alright. Hey, how about Chinese for dinner?"

"Sounds good."

"See you there."

"Brandon, I need to go to 7-Eleven for coffee."

"Okay, get Marc and Frankie."

"Coming!"

Tiffany waits 20 minutes to be sure they are gone. She comes into Grams's room, wearing gloves, she opens the funnel cake box and switches the funnel cake. She makes sure everything is the way Grams left it.

At church, things were going good. Joan sent a text to everyone about the double baby shower. There was an unexpected person at church.

"Marie! Look who is here."

"Tex? Our landlord?"

"Hi Tex, is something wrong?"

"I hope you don't mind, I decided to pay you guys a visit. And I need to discuss a few things with you."

"Sure, we are happy to have you visit our church. What would you like to talk about?"

"Not now. I will stop by after church."

"Okay. Well, I hope you like the service."

"Good morning, everyone! It's good to be in the house of the Lord. We have a guest with us so everyone greet him. Our call to Worship is Psalm 100. Arlene, can you come lead us in our first song?"

"Our first song is Blessed Assurance page 250. Tonya will be singing a solo called Come just as you are."

"Our announcements for this week are in the bulletin. Everything is the same. Will

Lynn and Thomas come and do the offering? Thank you!"

"Father, we ask that our offering be acceptable to you. May it be used to further your kingdom. In Jesus' name, Amen!"

"Our next song is What A Friend, page 300."

"The message for today is called, Being Childlike, open your Bibles to Matthew 18:3.

Tina, please close us in prayer. Everyone, have a great day!"

"Tex, if you would like to meet us at the house. We need to lock up."

"Sure, I will meet you there."

"Brandon, we need to quickly close up. Tex is meeting us at the house."

"Everything okay?"

"I don't know."

"Hey hon, we need to get going. The landlord is meeting us at the house,"

"Okay, Arlene, we can meet up on Tuesday about programs."

"That will be fine, just no Tiffany."

"Not a problem."

"Where is she today? She keeps begging me to be in the choir."

"She said she was sick."

"I hope she feels better."

"Alright, see you Tuesday."

"Are you ready, Marie? The boys are in the SUV."

"Yes, I'm coming."

Back at the house, Tex is waiting for the rest to come home before he begins.

"Would you like something to drink?"

"Do you have any lemonade?"

"Sure."

"Hi Tex, how are you?"

"Good. I loved the service." "Thank you!"

"Thanks for the lemonade."

"So what did you want to talk about?"

"You guys have been living here for 10 years. I wanted to offer you to buy it. Say $75,000."

"Yes!"

"Are you sure?"

"Yes!"

"I can help you apply for a mortgage. We can have the lawyers go over the

details."

"That's fine. Why are you selling it?"

"Well you've been excellent tenants, I just figured you could get a mortgage cheaper than what you are paying me rent. So, now that we got that out of the way, I am no longer with my girlfriend."

"Sorry to hear that."

"Joan, I know this sounds bad, but I know you've had a crush on me since you moved in and I always liked you. Would you go out with me sometime?"

(blushing)"Yes, I would love to."

"Great! Well that's all I needed to know."

"Hey, why don't you stay for dinner. We are ordering Chinese."

"I don't want to impose."

"It's not a problem."

"So, Tex ,how long have you liked my daughter?"

"Mom!"

"What? I'm nosey, I want to know."

"It's okay. I've liked her for a few years."

"Are you planning on marrying her?"

"Well, let's take things slowly and see where it goes."

"Okay. Mom, no more questions."

"Fine! I want pork fried rice and boneless spareribs. I will be upstairs."

"Please excuse her."

"She's okay. What are some things you like to do?"

"I like to go to the movies, go for walks, and go out to eat.

What about you?"

"I like to travel. Do you?"

"I never had the money. I went to Florida, Ohio, and California. That's it."

"Money is no object. I would pay."

"I would have to contribute something."

"That is up to you. I don't mind paying."

"I just don't want it to seem like I am using you."

"Well, I know you would never take advantage of me."

"Well, let's order dinner."

Upstairs........

"Hey, Scott."

"Yeah!"

"I can't eat any more, do you want them?"

"Yeah, I love funnel cake. Thank you."

It only took Scott 15 minutes to eat the remaining 3 funnel cakes. Now how long before the poison takes effect? Dinner went well. They all got to know Tex better. Joan and Tex set a date for next Friday night. Dinner.

All night Scott was up sick. Joan went to bed with a smile on her face. The guy she liked for a long time asked her out. Kym and Sam stayed up watching movies.

Grams read her Bible before going to bed. Tiffany was waiting for Grams to get sick.

Paul, Marc, and Frankie were up playing video games. Marie, Brandon, and Lynn were figuring out baby names. Lynn was excited that she was allowed to help.

MONDAY, SEPTEMBER 3, 1990

The sun was out. It looked like it was going to be a beautiful day. Loan had a busy day. She has to buy everything she needs for the double baby shower. She headed to the bathroom to take a shower. She has to push the door hard just to open it. Once the door was opened...

"OMG! SCOTT! SCOTT! OH NO! SOMEONE CALL 911! HELP!"

"What are you yelling about?"

"Mom, call 911."

"And what do I say is wrong?"

"Well...look?"

"OMG! What is hanging from his mouth?"

"I think it's his intestines."

"I'm going to be sick.'

"911 Where is your emergency?"

"2222 Logan Street."

"What's the emergency?"

"My roommate was found with his intestines hanging out of his mouth."

"Ma'am, this is for serious calls. You can be arrested for a false report."

"Look, I am being serious. Please send help!"

"EMS is on their way."

"Thank you!"

"What's going on, Aunt Joan?"

"There is something wrong with Scott. Can you go downstairs and let the ambulance in?"

"Sure."

"Thank you, Frankie."

Everyone started to get up. All wondering what the commotion was all about. Tiffany sees Grams, then sees Scott. Her plan was ruined! I will get her next time. She showed the paramedics where to go. The paramedics called the police. They were reporting this as a murder.

"Hello Pastor Wert, I am Detective Lamb and this is..."

"I remember you both."

"What happened?"

"Well, Scott was up sick all night. And this is how I found him this morning. That's all I know."

"Did he have any enemies, or did he have any problems with anyone?"

"Not that I know. Well on second thought, he and his brother really never got along."

"Do you know his name and where we can find him?"

"He lives at 120 Franklin Street. His name is Nevin Monroe."

-Okay, thank you. Who is meeting us at the hospital?"

"Brandon and Sam, will you come with me?"

"No problem."

"We will call when we know something."

"Okay, Mom."

"Oh, afterwards I have some baby shower errands to run.'

"Should Brandon take his truck?"

"No, I will need help. They can ride with me."

"See you later."

"Joan, can I borrow your laptop?"

"Why?"

"To start looking for a job and places to live."

"Yes, Marie knows the password."

"Thank you!'

"Now to ruin this baby shower."(Tiffany thinks to herself)"All eyes on me."

Her thoughts were interrupted by Marie handing her the laptop and putting the password in. Tiffany waits until Marie walks away before she goes through Joan's files. The plan is to cancel all the arrangements for the baby shower, as she pretends to look for work and a place to live.

"Where would Joan put her party plans at? Adult programs? Children's or teen ministries? Sunday school? No! Damn it! Where are those plans at?"

Tiffany went through all 200 of Joan's documents, down-loads, and pictures and found nothing. The evil one is pissed! Well, there is more than one way to ruin a baby shower. I know just what to do. The evil one thinks to himself. Her thoughts were interrupted by Paul.

"Hey ,babe. What are you doing?"

"Oh um....I thought I would get started on looking for a job and a place of our own."

"Great!"

"What are you doing today?"

"I thought we could visit my dad."

"You know Deb hates me."

"My dad is taking us out for lunch. No Deb."

"Where is he taking us?"

"To Very Best. They have the best food."

"Okay, what time?"

"He said to be ready at 11:00."

Meanwhile at the hospital....

"Excuse me! Can anyone tell me what is going on?"

"Who are you here with?"

"Scott Monroe."

"Friend or family?"

"I'm his roommate."

"I'm sorry I can only give information to his family."

"Nurse, I'm Detective Lamb, she is also his family's pastor. Give her any information you have."

"Okay, I will get the doctor."

"Thank you!"

"I am Dr. Winfield, I pronounced Mr. Monroe dead as soon as he came in."

"What did he die of?"

"We need to do an autopsy to be sure. What he ingested caused severe vomiting that caused what you walked in on. It doesn't look like he had a chance of surviving."

"Oh dear. Detective? Will you be telling Scott's brother?"

"I can tell the parents too."

"His parents are deceased."

"Well, then just the brother."

"Thank you!"

"All part of the job."

"What will happen to his body? He doesn't have life insurance."

"Then it will get cremated and thrown away."

"Oh no, I can't have that! I will pay and take care of it."

"The nurse will have some papers for you to sign."

"Alright. Brandon, call Jeff at Houck and Gofus funeral home."

"Will do."

"Houck and Gofus funeral home, Jeff speaking."

"Hey Jeff, it's Brandon the pastor at church. A friend of ours has died. We would like to use your funeral home. We will cover all costs."

"Great! What hospital?"

"Pottstown Memorial Medical Center. They are doing an autopsy."

"Scott Monroe."

"Okay, I will be speaking to you."

"Alright, Jeff. Joan, everything is all set up. When the autopsy is done, Jeff will come pick Scott up."

"Okay, let's go shopping. Sam calls home and tells them to order dinner for themselves. Marie knows where the money is."

"Marie, your mom said to order take out for dinner."

"Where are you guys?"

"We are just leaving the hospital now."

"So, you're headed shopping?"

"Yes!"

"For what?"

"I can't tell you. Your mom will kill me."

"I know she will. Have fun."

"Yeah right!"

"Where are we going?"

"Did she ask to find out?"

"No, I want to know if we are eating out?"

"Yes, after we go shopping."

"Sam, don't worry, you will eat."

"Fine!"

"Let's go to the party supply first then head to Sears for the baby furniture."

"Furniture?"

"Yes! The baby will be here soon, and we don't have any-thing."

"You don't have to, Joan."

"It's my first grandchild!"

"Well, thank you."

"Don't worry about it. My baby shower gift."

"Joan, let Kym and I buy the stroller and the car seat."

"What kind of stroller are you getting?"

"The kind that you can push from both sides. I like Graco.

I will let Kym know when I get home."

"Are you getting it today?"

"Since we are out. This way you can help me pick them out."

"Well here we are."

"What are we getting here?"

"Party, supplies, Game prizes, napkins, plates, silver-ware, cups, tablecloths."

"How many people are you expecting?"

"About 150 plus us."

"That's a big shower."

"It's for Marie and Celeste."

"Okay, I will get her gift today too."

"Well, I can help you."

"Great! There goes my bank account."

"Get her the same thing you're getting Marie."

"Sears is so expensive."

"The quality is worth it. I will pay half for them both. Will that help you out?"

"It's okay. I have the money. I'm just cheap."

"Okay, well they both will appreciate it."

"I hope so."

The rest of the day went well. Joan spent over $2,000 on baby stuff for Marie and Celeste, and another $1,000 on party stuff. Then they went to The Pottstown Diner for dinner.

Marie ordered pizza from Dominoes. The boys helped carry the furniture to the baby's room. The gifts and party supplies were taken to Joan's office at the church. Everything was coming together. Tiffany is already tired of hearing about the baby shower. Her luncheon with Bob did not go well. Bob refused to talk to Deb about them moving back. Paul is allowed but not Tiffany. Now she has to put up with this baby shower crap.

Everyone is exhausted. They all went to bed early. To-mor-row Brandon and Dan are setting up the baby's nurs-ery. Marie and Celeste have doctor's appointments. Joan needs to figure out funeral plans for Scott.

TUESDAY, SEPTEMBER 4,1990

Grams woke up excited. Last night Marie asked her and Lynn if they wanted to see the baby. Of course, she made them promise not to tell anyone the sex.

Joan is contacting people who knew Scott to tell them about his passing. She is planning a service for him on Friday. Something short.

"Everyone is up now...

"What time is your appointment, Marie?"

"10:00. I'm taking Grams and Lynn with. Maybe get lunch afterwards."

"Sounds good."

"What are your plans, Mom?"

"I need to contact people who knew Scott. There will be a service on Friday."

"That's before the baby shower."

"That way I can stay after and set up for Saturday."

"Isn't your date with Tex on Friday?"

"Yes, I will be ready. Scott didn't have many friends."

"Brandon and Dan are setting up the crib and stuff. Thank you very much. You didn't have to."

"It's my first grandchild. Of course, I needed to. Sam got you stuff, too."

"Sam bought something other than soda?"

"Yes. Well, I need to head to the church. Lots of work to do."

"Have a good day."

"You, too!'

Tiffany and the rest got up. Grams and Lynn are dressed and ready to go. Brandon was waiting for Dan to come.

"Morning, Marie. How are you?"

"I'm doing good. Thank you, Tiffany."

"Where is Aunt Joan?'

"She went to contact people for Scott."

"Okay, what is everyone doing today?"

"Celeste and I have doctor appointments. Brandon and Dan are putting together the baby's room. The boys are probably playing their video games. I'm not sure about Sam and Kym.

Grams and Lynn are coming with me."

"How far along are you?"

"About 6 months. Celeste and I have the same due date."

"Oh, that's nice."

Tiffany is so tired of hearing about the baby she is ready to scream. She just needs the perfect moment to put her plan in action.

At the police station, there are now 2 cases to solve. Detectives Lamb and Plump discuss both cases as forensics and the autopsy report is read on Scott.

"Hey Larry, what do you have for us?"

"Well, the same person who killed the last victim killed Mr.

Monroe."

"Are you sure?"

"Yes. On the box of funnel cake we found in the victim's room, was a 666 fingerprint."

"It's good to know we are dealing with one person. Anything from the coroner?"

"Yes. They found traces of boric acid and rat poison. That's why he was found with his intestines out of his mouth. Oh, his last meal was funnel cake."

"Boric acid and rat poison are white. It sounds like someone used them as the white powder for the funnel cake."

"Could be. Boric acid was also used in the other murder. It was put in the lotion."

"That's interesting."

"Thank you, Larry. We need to look into Tiffany Powers closer."

"Why her?"

"She is new to both households."

"So you think she is the killer?"

"Well, all of a sudden people are dying. We know she and Lori had problems.

But, I know nothing about her and Scott."

"Should we let the families know?"

"Not until we are sure. Anyway, I have Nevin Monroe coming in. He is Scott's brother. There he is. Mr. Monroe, please have a seat."

"Why was I called down here?"

"Sorry to have to tell you this, but your brother Scott was murdered yesterday."

"Good! I hate that asshole!"

"You didn't get along with your brother?"

"No! He was the favorite. My mom needed health benefits. I told him we would help pay it. He said no. He never helped with our mom, but knew her when he needed money. When our mother died, that bastard did not help pay for her funeral expenses, hell he didn't even show up for his own mother's funeral."

"Sorry to hear that. Where were you Sunday night?"

"I'm a suspect because I hated my brother?"

"No, I just have to ask."

"I was at Hahnemann Hospital in Philadelphia with my wife. She has bone marrow cancer. I wanted my brother to die, I didn't kill him."

"Do you know of anyone who may have wanted him dead?"

"Yeah! A lot of people. His best friend from high school, he slept with his wife.

His ex-girlfriend who he owes $10,000 to. People he works with call him an ass kisser. He acts like a big shot, like he is the best at everything. Take your pick."

"WOW! Write down the company he worked for and the people who have grudges against him."

"Then can I go?"

"Yes!"

"Thank God."

At the Wert house, Brandon and Dan are setting up the baby furniture. Tiffany and Paul are out trying to move back in with his dad.

"So, has Marie told you what she's having?"

"A girl."

"That's what we are having. What are you naming her?"

"Deja Marie Kwon."

"That's a pretty name. We are naming our daughter, Jenna Lynn Davis." "Nice!"

"How are things going with Tiffany and Paul living here?'

"Tough! Grams and her always fight. Grams calls her the devil and evil. Tiffany does not like the fact she cannot sleep with Paul or even be in each other's rooms."

"Oh wow! Where are they?"

"Who knows. Probably trying to find a place they can sleep together. Probably begging Paul's dad."

"How are you guys holding up with Scott's death?"

"Kind of shaken up. They are calling it a murder."

"Really?"

"Yes, because his intestines were hanging out of his mouth."

"Ewwwww! I just lost my appetite."

"Sorry!"

"Where is Aunt Joan?"

"She is getting ready for Scott's funeral on Friday."

"Wow, that's soon. Do you know what time?"

"No, I will let you know. It may just be us. He didn't have friends."

"He didn't?"

"His brother hates him. His best friend stopped talking to him because he slept with his wife. He owes his ex $10,000.The people at work call him the brown noser.

They hate him."

"That's sad."

"Yes, it is. So, do you think Marie will like it?"

"She'd better."

Tiffany and Paul decided to go to his dad's and talk to Deb face to face.

"What the hell are you doing here?"

"I just want to talk to you."

"I have nothing to say to you."

"Just hear me out. I know you think I killed Lori, but I didn't. I'm very sorry for everything I put you through."

"What do you want, Tiffany?"

"Can we move back in?"

"No! How dare you even think about it."

"Joan's place is nice, but she won't let us share a room."

"Look, I could care less what you're not allowed to do at Joan's. You never respected my rules and you want to move back in. Hell, NO!"

"Sooner or later you have to accept me in the family. Paul and I will be married."

"Well, good for you. I don't have to accept anything, and I do not have to let you live here. Now, leave."

"Fine, we will leave. Mark my words, I will be back here one day."

"Over my dead body."

"That can be arranged." Thought the evil one.

Everyone had such a busy day that they went to their rooms early. Tiffany was pissed that Deb said no. Joan was sad that only 3 people plus her family will be at the funeral Friday. Marie was happy with the way the baby's room turned out. Grams and Lynn were excited they got to see the baby first. Everyone slept peacefully.

WEDNESDAY, SEPTEMBER 5, 1990

The sun is out, the birds are singing. A beautiful day. At the Montgomery house they talked about Tiffany asking to move in.

"Good morning, hon! How did you seep?"

"I slept good. Did you know Tiffany was coming by to ask to move back in?"

"I knew they wanted to move back in. I didn't know she was asking you."

"You knew?"

"I took them to Very Best for lunch the other day. I didn't tell you because I already told them no."

"You still should have told me so I could be prepared for if they came by. Which they did. Thank you for saying no."

"I know how you feel about Tiffany and it wouldn't be right to go against you. I love you and don't want to hurt you in any way."

"Thank you! I love you too. What are your plans today? I'm doing yard work. The

plant is still closed for sterilization."

"I am finishing up cleaning the downstairs. I thought about taking that old paneling down and maybe sanding and painting the downstairs pretty blue. Maybe make a little seating area so if we are having company over, they don't have to come up here."

"It sounds good to me. What kind of furniture would you get?"

"I thought about a nice wicker set."

"Why don't we pick it out together? How about I help you instead of the yard?"

"I would love it if you would."

At the Wert house, Marie, Brandon and Joan are discussing Scott's funeral. Tiffany and Paul tried asking to share a room. The boys went to hang with friends. Lynn is playing with friends, and Grams went to sit on the porch.

"So, Mom, how did it go calling Scott's brother and friends?"

"Not good! His brother is glad he is dead. Out of 200people,only 2 are coming

Friday."

"Oh wow! He has no friends? I knew his brother hated him, just not like that."

"Nope! His brother is glad he is dead. His best friend wants nothing to do with him. The people he works with could care less. I had to beg the 2 that are coming."

"That's sad."

"Well, it explains why he was always home. I didn't know Nevin hated Scott that badly."

"Brandon, Nevin and Scott were always fighting as kids."

"That's crazy! They never got along?"

"Nope!"

"Aunt Joan, can we talk to you?"

"Sure, what is it?"

"What can we do to share a room?"

"Be married. I will not go against my beliefs for anyone."

"Why not? We are engaged; it's the same thing."

"No, it's not and I'm not changing my mind."

"Paul, can we get married now?"

-But, we hardly know each other."

"Do you love me?"

"Yes!"

"Do you want to spend your life with me?"

"Yes, but now!"

"Please?"

"Brandon, would you marry us?"

-

"Paul, you need to think this through. Marriage is a huge step. You shouldn't be pressured into it or get married to sleep with someone."

"Well, I do love her, and I did propose to her. So yes, I want to get married."

"Before I say yes, you need to have a week of marriage counseling. We start

Monday. Be at my office at 4:00 P.M."

"Okay. Thank you!"

"I'm not doing this wedding if I don't feel you're both ready."

"Don't worry, we are."

"Well your first assignment is 1) write down why you want to get married. Paul, write yours in front of Marie, and Tiffany in front of Joan. Not together! Give them both to Marie and she will put them in my office at the church."

"Why can't we do it together?"

"Because I want to be sure Paul is putting his honest thoughts and feelings into this and not what you tell him to put."

"I'm not like that! It's not fair!"

"It's my way or I don't do it."

"FINE!"

At the police station, Detective Lamb finds out some details about Tiffany Powers.

"Boy, you're here early!"

"I was doing some checks on Miss Powers."

"Well... when she was at Pansy House 2 people died. One was a girl she just had a fight with. Then a therapist, but there does not appear to be a connection between the therapist and Miss Powers. There is also a family whose house burned down. The bodies were never found."

"Never found? Like they vanished? Not even bones were found?"

"Nope!"

"WOW!"

"There is more..."

"More?"

"When she was 6, she was put in a psychiatric hospital. Her parents found her stabbing herself in the arms and legs. All because her parents were getting divorced. Then when she was 10,she tried to drown her sister in the family pool. She was tired of her sister being Mommy's favorite. When she was 16,a girl at school was trying to steal her boyfriend. Was found with her hands burned off, her private area sewn shut, and her lips cut off!"

"So violence seems to follow this chick?"

"Yes, it does. I bet if we keep digging, we will find some more things out about her."

"Sounds like a lot of long nights ahead of us."

"Yes, indeed! Who is she really? What is she hiding?"

"I hope we find out before something else happens."

"Me too!"

At the Montgomery house, things are looking up. All the paneling downstairs is off. Bob sanded the walls, cleaned up the woodwork. He had a plumber come in to give him an estimate on making the scrub tub section into a powder room so guests don't have to go upstairs. Bob and Debbie went to Home Depot to get paint and other things to fix the house up. They went to Friendly's for dinner, watched the Three Stooges, and went to bed.

Things went peaceful at the Wert house. Tiffany sat up planning her wedding. Paul kept thinking to himself; "What am I getting into?" Frankie and Mark were playing video

games. Sam and Kym went for a walk. Lynn and Grams watched movies. Aunt Joan was talking on the phone with Tex. Brandon and Marie went on a double date with her cousin, Bella, and her husband, Billy. They have a 2 year old daughter named Ashley who is autistic and a 1 year old son named Don. They haven't seen each other in a while and wanted to catch up. The evening ended well for everyone.

THURSDAY, SEPTEMBER 6,1990

It was raining very hard. People who lived near the rivers were being evacuated due to possible flooding. Joan, Brandon, Frankie ,Marc, and Paul went to open the church up to those who were displaced. They had 4 families. One family attended the church. They brought out cots and put each family in a Sunday school room. It's better than on the streets. Tiffany, Grams, Marie, and Lynn went to the store to pick up food for the families.

The latest report from the weather channel said the rain would last until evening. So far there have only been reports of minor flooding.

"Marie, what did you get?"

"Different types of chips, large hoagies, soda, snacks, water, macaroni and potato salad, coleslaw, and spaghetti for dinner with rolls and salad."

"I cannot believe you spent $500 on people you don't know."

"Well, we can't let them starve. It's the right thing to do. Besides, Jesus would want us to."

"I mean it's not like they are homeless and have nothing. And there is minimal flooding."

"No one knows what God is going to do. One minute nice and sunny, the next severe thunderstorms."

"God doesn't control everything! Come on, Joan, Mother Nature controls the weather."

"Genesis 1:1, In the beginning, God created the Heavens and the earth. That means everything. Didn't you say you were a Christian, Tiffany?"

"I am, Joan. I just don't believe as strictly as you do."

"Well, what do you believe?" asks Marie.

"Look...I believe in God. That Jesus died on the cross for my sins. I know the

Bible is real and that Jesus loves me."

"You don't sound convincing."

"I told you she was a liar, a fake, and a killer!"

"Mom, now stop. She's entitled to believe her way. Doesn't mean anything."

"Yes, it does!" Look at that look she's giving me!"

Tiffany gave Grams a devilish grin. Her eyes glowing red.

"You have no power here, Satan!"

"Now that is enough, Mother! Go in the kitchen and start cutting the hoagies. Tiffany and Marie, set up the other food. Boys, set up the plates, silverware, cups, and napkins. Brandon, tell the families lunch is done. And can you pray?"

"No problem. Everyone, before we get lunch, let's bow our heads for prayer.

"Father, we thank you for this food. We ask that each family be able to return to their homes. Bless the hands who put this all together. In Jesus' name I pray, Amen."

Everyone was served lunch. They were all grateful for the food. The rain stopped by evening. It was safe for the families to return home. One family tried to give the Werts money. They wouldn't take it. The family stayed to clean up and get food ready for tomorrow's funeral.

While they were getting ready for Friday, Joan and Marie decided to talk to Tiffany about her faith.

"Hey, Tiffany! I don't mean to be pushy about my faith or your faith. We seem to believe differently."

"Like how?"

"Well, you believe in sex before marriage. I don't. You are all about you. I help people. I'm not sure you really believe."

"So! The old bitch finally got to you? Just because I don't believe the way you do, doesn't mean I don't believe."

"Don't ever call my mother a bitch. And you're right, it doesn't mean you don't believe. Tell me this, when did you accept Jesus as your Savior?"

The evil one was ready to explode. He wanted to kill Joan at that moment. But that would ruin his plan.

"I don't remember; I was very young."

"Most people can tell you where they were, how old they were, and how they felt."

"Just because I can't remember doesn't mean I'm not saved."

"True. I will be watching you!"

"Are we done? I want to go home and plan my wedding."

"You will have to walk. We have to set up for the funeral tomorrow."

"FINE! I will stay and help."

"Okay, can you put the pictures on the stands, then we will be almost done."

"Mom, is everything alright?"

"Something is off about Tiffany. I don't know what it is exactly. But we need to be careful with her."

"Not you, too? Grams finally got you thinking."

"No! It's how she's been acting, how she talks. Plus the conversation I just had with her."

"About what?"

"I asked her when she was saved. She said she doesn't remember, that she was very young."

"Well that's one I haven't heard. Most people remember details. But it doesn't mean she is not saved."

"That's what I said, and I know it doesn't. She had this evil look in her eyes. Just be careful, and don't be too trusting."

"Okay, Mom. But you and Grams are going too far."

"Just be careful and let's hope I am wrong."

"Yes, Mom, I will

They were all done and decided to go to Taco Bell for dinner. They all were tired and just wanted to relax and unwind. When they got home, they all went to bed, except for Tiffany. Her mind wouldn't shut down. She had to plan her next kill. Who does the evil one want the most? The plan with Grams failed. He was really pissed off at Joan. Talking to his chosen one about Jesus. How dare she, Joan is of course the obvious choice. But Tiffany has someone else in mind. Someone who has stolen her spotlight one too many times. The evil one told her to stick to the plan, Joan was next. Finally, she was able to sleep. She slept peacefully. Dreaming of eliminating her next victim.

FRIDAY, SEPTEMBER 7,1990

A sad day at the Wert house. They will be saying their farewells to their long time family friend, Scott. It should be a short service, only 2-3 other people are coming and that's because Joan begged them. They all were getting ready to go. All were very upset except for Tiffany who is angry. This should be Isabell's funeral. But she will get her. And now Joan is asking questions. Then there is Marie who keeps stealing her spotlight. She was already on to her next victim.

Celeste and her husband were getting ready for the funeral. Dan really didn't like him. He considered Scott a creep.

The Montgomery's really didn't want to go. They felt bad that he had no family or friends. Plus, Debbie promised to help set up for the baby shower after. Joan is expecting 150 people outside of the family, so about 200 people. So Joan will need all the help she can get.

Everyone got to the church early. There really wasn't anything to set up. But just in case someone changed their minds to come. At 10:00 people started coming. Two people he worked with. Of course, the family and the Montgomery family. Celeste and her family. And unexpectedly his brother and sister-in-law, Nevin and Mandy.

"I wasn't expecting to see you?

"Mandy forced me to come."

"Well, let's get started. Brandon, I will do the service. Marie, please read Psalm

23 and pray?"

"Psalm 23.Let's pray.

"Father, we pray for those here today and ask for peace. Bless this final service for Scott Monroe. In Jesus' name I pray, Amen!"

"Thank you, Marie. Well, to be honest, we did not expect to see his brother, Nevin. I promise to try and make this short. Arlene, can you lead us in the song, "What a friend?"

As Arlene led the song, Tiffany sat and thought about her next victim. Her hatred for Joan grew stronger each day.

"Thank you! I know some of you didn't care for Scott. But if anyone has anything they would like to share, please just stand and speak?"

"My name is Chase. At one time we were good friends. I got up at 3 A.M. took him to work and picked him up. He never said thank you or offered gas money. Then he slept with my wife and got her pregnant."

"Okay, thank you! Anyone else?"

"My name is Connie, I worked with the back stabber. He went and told the boss everything I said, and I got fired. All because he wanted my job. He felt he could do better than me .He walked around like a big shot. No one likes him."

"Well, um... Anyone else?"

"I'm Nevin, his brother. First I want to say, I mean no disrespect to you and your family. Thank you for doing this. But my brother was an ass. He took money from our mom, never helped take care of our parents when they got sick. He has no friends except your generous family. I hope he rots in hell!"

"Um... Thank you! Well let's finish up. I don't know if Scott was saved. He kept to himself a lot. But I want you all to know that there is still time for you to be saved and have that assurance of going to heaven. There is only one way; John 3:5,Jesus answered and said to him, Most assuredly I say to you, unless one is born again, he cannot see the kingdom of God. The only way we can go to heaven when we die is by accepting Jesus as our Savior. Brandon please close in prayer."

"Father, I pray that we all see that we need you in our lives. In Jesus' name, we pray, Amen! Arlene close us in song."

"Let's end with victory in Jesus."

"Nevin! I'm sorry for your loss. I know you hated him."

"Joan, I have nothing against you or your family. Scott and I never got along, and you know that. But I hold none of it against you. Please keep in touch with me."

"You know I will. Here is my number, 484-555-6421."

"Thank you."

"Hey, Mom, that was quick."

"Well those people didn't want to be here. Plus did you hear what they were saying about him?"

"Yes! You did the best you could. What do you want me to help with?"

"Nothing! Actually, why don't you and Celeste go out for a few hours."

"Are you sure?"

"Yes!"

"Okay, if you're sure. Celeste, let's go to lunch and shopping."

"Doesn't Aunt Joan need our help?"

"I think they are setting up for tomorrow and don't want us here."

"Gotcha! Where do you want to go?"

"Let's go to the King of Prussia Mall. We can eat and shop."

"Okay, but I'm driving. You drive crazy like your mother."

"Thank you for the compliment."

As the girls went to King of Prussia Mall. Everyone else helped get ready for tomorrow's baby shower.

"What would you like me to do, Joan?"

"I want 2 chairs with blue and pink balloons. Then I want to have a table by each chair for the gifts. I want them both to have their own table. They will have their name on each. With twisted blue and pink streamers hanging down. I'm sorry if it's a lot for you, Deb."

"It's okay. Bob can help me."

"Great! Thank you. Tiffany and Paul! Can you both set up 20 tables with 10 chairs at each, 10 tables on each side. Pink and blue tablecloths. Like Pink, then blue all the way up the row. I also have decorations in the bags."

"No problem, Aunt Joan."

"Thank you both. Kym and Sam, can you set up the table for drinks and one for the dinnerware. Silverware, cups, plates, and napkins. There are blue and pink baskets for them. As well as decorations."

"How many people are you setting up for?"

"Um...200 people, that includes us."

Just then, Joan receives a phone call that changes her evening plans.

"Hey Tex, what's up?"

"I was wondering if we can do something simple tonight? I had a long day."

"Well I was having a cookout for everyone helping me set up for tomorrow. Want to join us?"

"Are you sure? This is not what I had in mind for a first date. I feel bad now."

"Don't worry about it. I had a long day too. This funeral was interesting."

"Why do you say that?"

"Well, first Scott's brother and family came, and had some unkind words to say about Scott. His best friend was here, and we found out he got his wife pregnant. Then a co-worker came and said Scott purposely had her fired to steal her job. This was all during the family and friends share time."

"Wow! That's a lot to take in at one time. So I will meet you at your place."

"Say about 3?"

"No problem."

"Hey, Mom, what's up?"

"Well, I need you and Dan to pick up food for a cookout today. Do you think we should invite Bella and Billy?"

"Um... don't you have that date with Tex? And Marie and Bella get along great!

"He's coming to our house. I am going to call Bella."

'Do you want us to get chicken, hot dogs, sausage, and hamburgers with all the trimmings?'

"Yes, sounds good. Hey Billy, is Bella there?"

"Sure, Aunt Joan. Bella! It's Aunt Joan."

"Hi, Aunt Joan. Everything okay?"

"Yes. We are having a cookout at 3 and would love it if you, Billy, and the kids would join us and come to the baby shower tomorrow?"

"I don't know Aunt Joan, Ashley is in a mood."

"I understand, but we don't get to see you guys and I know it would mean everything to Marie and me. If people don't like how Ashley is then they can leave. You are family."

"Okay and we will come tomorrow. Is it for Marie?"

"Marie and Celeste."

"Celeste and I don't get along. But I will come for Marie."

"See you later. Thank you."

"Everyone! Thank you all for staying to help me. All are welcome to my house afterwards for a cookout. Frankie and Marc, can you set up and decorate the dessert table.

Also I have some signs to hang up. Can you help me with that?"

"Sure, Aunt Joan."

"Thank you both. Bob and Sam, I have a caterer coming. Can you both set up all the food warmers?"

"Shouldn't they have their own food warmers?"

"Sam, those places use those metal things that don't keep the food warm evenly.

Please just do what I ask."

"Joan, are you okay?"

"Yes, Deb, I am fine. Why?"

"You all of a sudden are having an unplanned cookout. You seem out of sorts."

"Well, Tex called and said he just wants to do something simple. And I am not comfortable being alone with him yet."

"Wait! Did I miss something? You and the landlord?"

"I forgot to tell you. He is selling us the house and we are dating. Him and his girlfriend broke up and we both have liked each other for a long time."

"Well take it slow and get to know each other before you do anything serious. I understand you do not want to be alone with him yet. You both really don't know each other like that."

"Thank you, Deb."

"Anytime, my friend."

Everything was done. They all went back to the Wert house where Celeste and Marie started to marinade the meats and prepare all the food.

"So, how broke are we?"

"We had a lot of fun. Celeste and I bought stuff for us. We will go shopping for the babies after we see what we get tomorrow."

"Sounds good. Before I forget, Bella and Billy were invited."

"I love Bella and her family. Ashley is so adorable, and Don reminds me of his grandfather. Bella and Celeste do not get along. This should be interesting."

"Well, our family gatherings always are. I need to get the grills ready. Dan, can you help me with the grills and the cooking? Frankie, Marc, and Paul, can you set up the tables and chairs? And get the coolers ready."

"We just did all that work and now we have to do more! Are we getting paid?"

"You're being fed. That's good enough, Frankie."

"FINE!"

Everything was set to go. All were having a great time. Deb slayed away from Tiffany. Well, everyone avoided Tiffany. Tiffany didn't care. They all can go to hell as far as she is concerned, This gives her time to get her next project thought out. She had it mostly planned out in her head. Just a few details to figure out. Her thoughts were interrupted by Tex showing up and talking about the baby shower.

"Hey, everyone, how is it going?"

"Good. Everything is all set up for tomorrow. We just need to figure out how to get Marie and Celeste there at the same time."

"Well, Dan and I can pick up Marie on our way to the church. That way Brandon can help you with everything."

"Sounds like a plan. Thank you. Call me when you are on your way."

"No problem."

"Aunt Joan, can we go swimming?"

"Isn't it a little chilly for swimming?"

"Please...we are hot!"

"Okay, but check with Celeste and Bella."

"I will."

"Celeste, Bella, Dan, and Billy! I want you to meet Tex. We are starting to date and he is selling us the house. Tex, I know you met Celeste and Dan, Bella is my niece and this is her husband."

"Nice going, Aunt Joan!'

"Thank you, Bella. How have you all been doing?"

"We are doing good. Ashley has her ups and downs. She has a great team that works with her. We found a preschool that will work with her a few hours a day. Don wears glasses now. He likes to try and help his dad work on cars. The garage is doing well. We now have 5 bays, and 5 employees. We still

have the car club. Hondas are still my favorite. How have you been doing? Well, by the smile on your face, I think I have my answer. Is Grams staying out of trouble?"

"I am very happy and am glad you guys are doing great. We need to have you all over more. Ashley is getting big. She looks older than she really is. She is beautiful. Grams never stays out of trouble."

"I hear that a lot. She is only 3. She is a handful and sometimes Don acts up with her. So Tex, tell me about you? What are your interests with my aunt?"

"Bella!"

"It's okay, Joan. She doesn't know me. It's nice that you have people who only want what's best for you. So, to answer your question, I am a landlord with 100 properties. I take care of all of them. All are kept up to code and I fix things when they go wrong. I love to travel, love kids, I am saved. My intentions are to help your aunt buy this house, and to get to know her. And hopefully have a long, happy relationship."

"She has a huge family, we are always around. She is the pastor of a church. Will you be there for her through the ups and downs and understand when she can't just up and be with you?"

"I am a landlord, so when a problem happens at one of my properties there will be times that I have to cancel plans for that reason. So yes, I will understand she has a busy life. But at least with her life I can be a part of everything. Do I have your approval now?"

"Yes, welcome to the crazy house!"

"Thank you! What is wrong with Ashley that she needs special classes and help?"

"She is autistic. I love her just the way she is. I don't want your pity."

"I wasn't going to pity you. I just wanted to know. I know someone who works with autistic children. If you ever feel burned out or just need to get another opinion, let me know and I will call my friend. She has been doing this for 20 years."

"I will think about it."

The cookout lasted a few more hours. Everyone helped with cleaning up. It was a long day and tomorrow was another long day. They all went to bed early. Except Tiffany, her thoughts just kept going around and around. She couldn't wait to put her plan into action. This will be new territory for her.

SATURDAY, SEPTEMBER 8,1990

Baby shower day! Everyone is excited! Except, Frankie and Marc. They could care less about what Marie is having, another person living there. Plus they do all the work anyway. They are going for the food. Paul can't wait to see everyone and eat. And Tiffany is very excited about today.

"How are we doing this?"

"Mom, it doesn't start until 2 p.m. Plenty of time for details. What would you like for breakfast?"

"You know what, you don't have to be rude to me about it! I'm tired of being the last to know. And I want nothing from you."

"Mom, I can't tell you with Marie around. We will discuss it when we get there. Now, what would you like to eat?"

"You're right. I didn't think about that. I want pancakes, sausage, and coffee."

"Okay, then. Are we good now?"

"Yes, now shut up and feed me."

"Morning Isabell, morning Aunt Joan!"

"It was until you came down."

"Mom! Not today! Boy you're extremely happy today, Tiffany."

"Normally when a sour puss is happy, it means they got laid."

"Mother!"

"What?!That's an old saying!"

"It's okay. I wish I got laid. I'm just excited to hear what Marie and Celeste are having. Plus see all those gifts!"

"Don't steal anything."

"What would I do with baby gifts?"

"Sell them for money."

"Can we please just get along? I've done nothing to deserve this."

"I will give you one more chance to prove me wrong. And will be nice for today." "That's all I'm asking."

"Morning everyone! Isn't this a beautiful day?"

"Morning, Marie. What time is Celeste picking you up?"

"About 1:15."

"Just so you are there on time."

"Mom, don't worry. I wouldn't miss it for anything."

"Well, the rest of us will be there at 12 noon to help the caterers set up."

"Okay.""

"Tiffany, Mom, Paul, Lynn, Marc, and Frankie will ride with me. Sam and Kym will ride with Brandon. Well it's 9 A.M. let's get breakfast done and cleaned up. And get this party started."

"What are we having?"

"Grams wants pancakes and sausage."

"If I offer to cook, can we add hash browns?"

"You're going to cook for all of us, Frankie?"

"Yes, Aunt Joan. You need a break, I'm worried about you. Besides, we haven't had a big family breakfast in like forever."

They had a nice family breakfast, got everything cleaned up. It was 11:30 time to head to the church.

"Come on, Tiffany, time to go."

Coming up from the basement, "Is it okay if I meet you there? It's a beautiful day for a walk."

"Why were you in the basement?"

"I heard a noise and wanted to check it out. It was nothing.

So, can I walk?"

"Is Paul going with you?"

"You will need his help. Besides, I need to learn how to get around on my own sooner or later. Besides, we may not make it and go to a hotel. I'm trying to respect your rule."

"Good point and thank you. It's a half hour walk. Are you sure?'

"Yes. If I get tired or lost, I will call for a ride."

"Okay I have enough help."

"Thanks!"

"All right let's go! Marie, see you there. Love you!"

"Love you, too!"

At 12, Marie called Celeste to make sure what time she was coming. She was told it was 1:00. At 1:00, Tiffany got to the party.

"Hi, everyone."

"What took you so long?"

"I helped an old lady change her flat tire."

"That's why you're all dirty and sweaty?"

"Yes!"

At the Wert house...

"Marie! It's Celeste, time to go! Hello! Hey where are you hiding?"

She checked every room of the house. The basement, attic, outside. She noticed her keys, and purse were on the table. Her shoes and sweater were gone.

"Where's Marie?"

"I don't know. I checked the whole house. No Marie. Her keys, purse, and phone were on the table. Let me call my aunt."

"Celeste, where are you guys? People are showing up."

"Marie is not here."

"Enough with the games and get over here."

"What did she say?"

"She thinks I'm playing a game and said to get to the church."

"Well, let's go."

"Maybe Marie decided to find her own way there. She likes to make a grand entrance."

They get to the church and no Marie.

"Where's Marie?"

"Isn't she here?"

"Stop joking Celeste! Go get her! Everyone is waiting."

"Aunt Joan, we went to the house to pick her up and she wasn't there. We went in and searched the whole house. And no Marie. Her keys, phone, and purse were on the counter. She called me at 12 to see when I was coming."

"What's going on? Where is Marie?"

"We don't know, Brandon. She wasn't there. We searched the whole house. Her keys and everything are on the counter yet."

"Something is wrong. Maybe we should call the cops."

"I will call Mom. Just relax. I am sure she just wants to make a grand entrance."

"Hello, Pottstown Police Department, how may I direct your call?"

"Can I speak to someone in missing persons?"

"Hold please!"

"Detective Bowers speaking."

"I want to report my wife missing."

"Okay, how long has she been missing?"

"The last time someone spoke to her was 12 noon today."

"Sir, it's only been a few hours. Maybe she went shopping."

"Look, my wife is 6 months pregnant. Her keys, purse, and phone are on the counter. She should be at her baby shower with her friends and family."

"Okay. What is your address?"

"I would have to meet you there, I am at the baby shower."

"I will come to you, no one is allowed to leave. I need to speak to everyone there."

"Okay. It's One Way to Heaven Church on Gay Street. I am Pastor Kwon."

"Okay, we will be there in a few."

"The police are coming, no one is to leave. Keep an eye on Tiffany and Paul."

"Let's not say too much until they come."

"Okay, Mom."

"Joan, is everything okay?"

"Deb, keep this between you and me for now."

"Sure."

"Marie is missing. The police are on their way."

"Joan, seriously?"

"I am serious. Celeste went to pick her up and she wasn't there. Her keys, phone, and purse were on the counter."

"OMG!"

"SHH!"

"Sorry, so the police really are coming?"

"Yes, no one can leave. So keep an eye on Tiffany and Paul."

"Sure!"

The police walk in and Tiffany tenses up a little.

"I'm Detective Bowers, I'm looking for Pastor Kwon."

"That's me. This is my mother-in-law, Joan, and her niece, Celeste."

-Who was the last to see or speak with your wife?"

"Celeste, Marie called her at 12 to see when she was coming.

"That's not true!"

"What do you mean, Mom?"

"Remember, Tiffany left after us. She got here at 1."

"Where is Tiffany?"

"She is the one in the black dress."

"Tiffany?"

"Yes?"

"I'm Detective Bowers from missing persons. Can I ask you some questions concerning Mrs. Kwon?"

"Who is that?"

"The pastor's wife is missing, Marie Kwon."

"I only knew her first name. Marie is missing?"

"Yes, when did you last see her?"

"When I left the house at 11:30 she was still home."

"And what time did you arrive here?"

"At 1. Am I a suspect?"

"I have to ask everyone who last saw or spoke to the victim. It took you an 1

1/2 hour to get here from where?"

"Well I walked from Lee Avenue."

"Lee Ave is maybe a 30 minute walk. Where were you the other hour?"

"I helped an old lady change her tire."

"Okay, I will need to verify that."

"How? I didn't know the woman. She needed help and I helped her. Well I tried.

I stayed with her until AAA came."

"On what street?"

"The bottom of Lee Avenue."

"That's all for now."

"Pastor Kwon, where is Celeste?"

"Next to my mother-in-law by the food."

People were starting to wonder what was going on. Joan told everyone what was happening.

"Can I have everyone's attention please! I'm sorry to have to say this. Marie is missing. However, there is a lot of food,

please eat up. Some may be asked questions. Thank you all for coming and for your patience."

"Joan, I'm so sorry. If there is anything we can do just let us know."

"Thank you, Arlene. I hate to ask, but, when we leave with the detective, can you and the others clean up and lock up?"

"Don't worry about a thing. Focus on finding Marie."

"Thank you!""

As Detective Bowers is talking to Celeste, Sam, Kym, Grams, Frankie, Marc, Lynn, Bella, Billy, and Paul, Joan approaches.

All at once, "Why are we finding out this way? What's going on? Where's Marie?

Is this a joke?"

"One at a time, please!"

"What the hell is going on?"

"Mom and everyone! Celeste went to pick Marie up and she was not there. They searched the whole house and no Marie. Her keys, phone, and purse were on the counter. She was there at 11:00 when Tiffany left. And Celeste spoke to her at noon.

This is not a prank. The detective is going to be asking questions. Be honest with him."

"She's my granddaughter and I find out this way?"

"Mom, we had to keep it quiet so Tiffany wouldn't leave before the detective got to speak to her."

"So, you think she did it?"

"Mom, I don't know what to think. I mean a 30 minute walk turned into 1 1/2. And she claims she helped change a tire. Does she look dirty to you? And I started thinking about some things, and maybe you are right. Something is definitely off with her."

"Now you believe me? Now that it is your child, you believe me? You defended her and called me crazy! How dare you!"

"Grams, this is not the place nor the time. Let's focus on finding Marie and pray her and the baby are okay."

"You're right, Frankie. But the detective needs to investigate Tiffany."

"Detective, I have some things to tell you."

"And you are?"

"Isabell Wert, Marie's grandmother."

"Sorry you are going through this. What would you like to say?"

"See that girl Tiffany?"

"Yes, I already spoke to her."

"Ever since she got here, there's been death and drama. When she lived at Bob and Deb's, Deb's sister died. They were constantly fighting and arguing. Then she moves in with us and last week Scott dies and now Marie is missing."

"I promise I will look into everything you have told me. Thank you for the information."

"Pastor Kwon, let's go to the station and figure out our next move."